Hortense in Exile

OTHER BOOKS BY JACQUES ROUBAUD
IN ENGLISH TRANSLATION

Our Beautiful Heroine
Hortense Is Abducted
Some Thing Black
The Great Fire of London

Jacques Roubaud

HORTENSE IN EXILE

Translated by
Dominic Di Bernardi

Dalkey Archive Press

Originally published by Éditions Seghers; © 1990 by Éditions Seghers
English translation © 1992 by Dominic Di Bernardi
First American Edition

Library of Congress Cataloging-in-Publication Data
Roubaud, Jacques.
  [Exil d'Hortense. English]
  Hortense in exile / Jacques Roubaud: translated by Dominic Di
Bernardi.
  Translation of: Exil d'Hortense.
  I. Title.
PQ2678.O77E9713   1992
843'.914—dc20   91-29759
ISBN: 1-56478-001-5

Partially funded by grants from The National Endowment for the Arts,
The Illinois Arts Council, and the French Ministry of Culture.

Dalkey Archive Press
Fairchild Hall
Illinois State University
Normal, IL 61761

*Printed on permanent/durable acid-free paper and bound in the United
States of America.*

CONTENTS

Part Four: *Perhaps You Were Hoping for a Graceful Return to Days of Yore?*

Part Five: *In Which We Contemplate Elementary Laws*

Part Six: *The Classic Tearful Parting from the Attractions of a Novel Nearing Its End*

MAIN CHARACTERS OF THE DRAMA

At Home

HORTENSE, heroine.
LAURIE, redhead, friend of Hortense, mother of Carlotta.
CARLOTTA, redhead, Laurie's daughter.
OPHELIA, Carlotta's cat.
INSPECTOR BLOGNARD, our greatest detective.
INSPECTOR ARAPÈDE, Blognard's assistant.
JIM WEDDERBURN, Laurie's partner.
THE AUTHOR.

In Poldevia

PRINCE GORMANSKOÏ, alias Airt'n, Premier Presumed Prince of Poldevia, Hortense's lover and fiancé.
PRINCE AUGRE, Gormanskoï's foe.
PRINCE ACRAB'M, Gormanskoï's friend.
ALEXANDRE VLADIMIROVITCH, Cat Prince.
CYRANDZOÏ, Pony Prince, friend of Carlotta.
FATHER RISOLNUS, abbot of Léthème, theoretician of rhythm.
ALCIUS, Usurping Reigning Prince, second husband of Gertrude.
GERTRUDE, Gormanskoï's mother.
MISTERS T. AND T., secret agents in Alcius's hire.
WHORTENSE, the Wrong (or Fake) Hortense, Augre's accomplice.

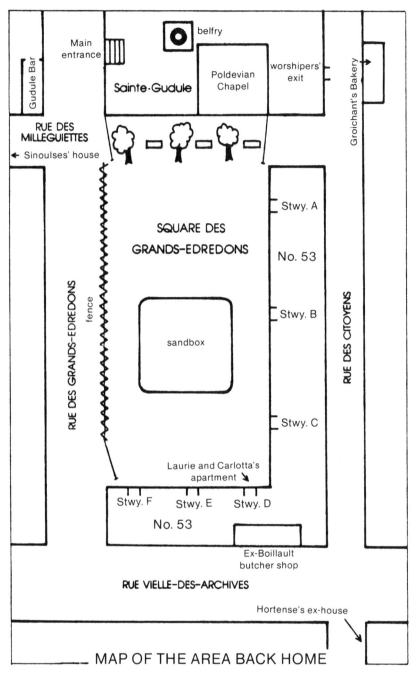

MAP OF THE AREA BACK HOME

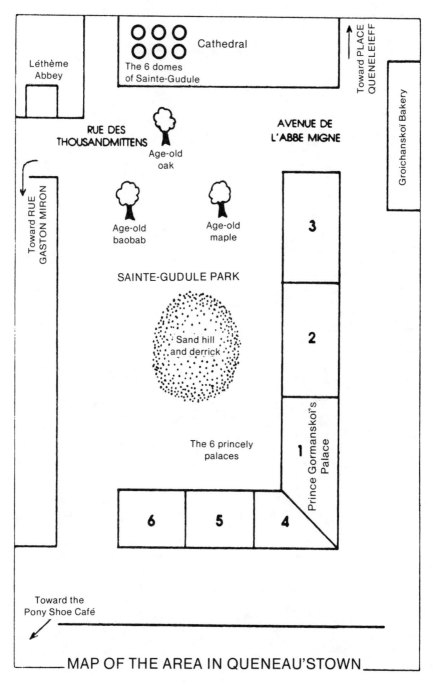

Léthème Abbey

Cathedral

The 6 domes of Sainte-Gudule

Toward PLACE QUENELEIEFF

Groichanskoï Bakery

RUE DES THOUSANDMITTENS

Age-old oak

AVENUE DE L'ABBE MIGNE

Toward RUE GASTON MIRON

Age-old baobab

Age-old maple

3

SAINTE-GUDULE PARK

Sand hill and derrick

2

The 6 princely palaces

1

Prince Gormanskoï's Palace

6

5

4

Toward the Pony Shoe Café

MAP OF THE AREA IN QUENEAU'STOWN

Part One

A Matter-of-fact Introduction to This Heart-throbbing Tale of Adventure

Chapter 1

Bathing with Hortense

Alexandre Vladimirovitch sprang upward. His right forepaw nimbly rapped the tip of the doorknob. The laws of mechanics, instituted long ago by Archimedes during one of his baths in Syracuse, were set into motion. The door began to open. Dropping back to the floor, Alexandre Vladimirovitch shoved the door along with his left forepaw. After crossing the threshold, he used his trained eyes to check that the premises were free of spies, assassins, and mice; then he drew aside to let Hortense pass.

Hortense stepped into the palace bathroom. She headed for the large semicircular bathtub and turned the six water faucets: VERY HOT, HOT, LUKEWARM, COLD, FREEZING. From the sixth and last faucet flowed a current alternating between SCALDING and ICY thirty-seven times per second; each thin stream ran into the gilded bronze master faucet, creating a powerful, frothy, steady thrust. Hortense kept adjusting them until she got just the right temperature. The bathtub started to fill.

The cubical bathroom covered a 317-square-meter surface. Three sides were in black marble, the other three in white. There were mirrors; a low, 41-square-meter bathtub, made of basalt and lava; black, white, and red towels bearing the Prince's effigy; bars of scented soap; stoppered bottles containing balsamic oils for bubble baths; bobby pins and combs, etc. Hortense placed on the floor the "cordless" mother-of-pearl snail-phone that she had been holding in her hand, kicked her slippers across the room, undid her belt. Her bathrobe slid down from her shoulders, momentarily detained by her breasts,

3

reluctant to show themselves, and then likewise by her hips. She was naked. Stepping up onto the hypersensitive electronic scale, accurate, precise, and reliable, she stood very straight so she wouldn't throw off the reading, which flashed up in red fluorescent figures on the white wall facing her: 124 pounds, 9 ounces—i.e., four ounces heavier than the day before. ("Chocolate, chocolate," she reflected.)

Stepping off the scale, she extended her left foot down into the tub and tested the water with her big toe. The water's message, penetrating her foot, climbed her leg and continued along her 171-centimeter length until it reached Hortense's summit, up amid her dense, gossamer, very soft light brown locks: it communicated perfection. Hortense quivered with pleasure and set her foot on the bottom of the tub. The water rose almost to her calf.

A laudable concern for symmetry led her to slip her second foot into the tub, and she held her pose for a moment as she got used to the warmth. Mentally she readied the various regions of her body for the water's imminent contact and pressure, which in all probability would equal the weight of the displaced liquid (four more ounces than yesterday! "Chocolate, chocolate," she re-reflected). This is one of those so very pregnant truths from the world of physics which are not given enough thought at bathtime.

Alexandre Vladimirovitch settled elegantly on the rim of the tub in the special cat's seat. All bathtubs belonging to beautiful young women have a cat seat. It's located at the one and only spot which remains splash-free while these women move about in the water. Between the tub's gray basalt and the black marble of the three walls, Alexandre Vladimirovitch's dark, gray-black fur, shot through with a bare hint of blue (but a blue so deeply blue it was practically not blue anymore, but almost red), discreetly blended in, as always, with its surroundings. In addition, he had white whiskers and gold-flecked pupils.

His eyes never left Hortense. After soaping at length between

4

her toes, Hortense had moved up to her knees which, as on every morning, she studied with a puzzled look of reproach. Despite her fiancé the Prince's repeated and persuasive arguments, to her mind they epitomized her failure to achieve genuine beauty: too round, she thought, and "goofy-looking," as it were. She punished them with neglect and proceeded to the milky caramel of her thighs. In actual fact, her thighs were not fundamentally different in color from the other parts of her body; but it's clear that the caramel/thigh association has a greater descriptive power than the conjunction of "caramel" with "calf," for instance. This explains why it happens to take priority.

As we've already stated, Alexandre Vladimirovitch's eyes never left Hortense, and he followed the sensual progress of her self-soaping. "I wonder," thought Hortense, "what he might be thinking while watching me like that every morning?"

"What I'm thinking," thought Alexandre Vladimirovitch, who like all cats (excellent cognitivists that they are), but with even greater clarity due to his personal qualities and his noble rank (he was a prince), hadn't any problem at all decoding human brain waves: they're so slow, so elementary, not to mention so awfully encumbered with language.

So then, Alexandre Vladimirovitch thought, "What I'm thinking is how remarkably bare of fur her whole body is; no doubt, according to human criteria, if I take into account the appraisal of the Prince, who's a connoisseur, Hortense's scanty fur is placed on her person correctly, strategically, and with a touch of charm, I grant. But, first: the awkward discontinuity between fur and non-fur, a trait shared by all human beings regardless of sex, is a regrettable defect in harmony; second, if this fur has an erotic purpose, and this is assuredly so in Hortense's case, how does it happen that a large part of said fur serves in fact no practical purpose? Is it not a deceitful lure, a disappointing simulacrum? The fur of our females, by contrast, serves so very many . . ."

5

So ran Alexandre Vladimirovitch's thoughts, along with a good number of others, at a cat's mental speed which is too swift to be followed, exceeding the velocity of all material, corpuscular, and wave particles, and thus disproving the most (wrongly) unchallenged principles of Inchtin's Relativity and Max (le Planque)'s Theory of Quotas.

Hortense's relationship with the Prince's cat was still marked by a slight, but noticeable discomfort. He was always very courteous, purring politely whenever she petted him; he fulfilled the responsibilities of his office punctually, parsimoniously, and with virtuosity, but some hint of a misunderstanding between the two, dating back to when they first met, persisted despite everything. Alexandre Vladimirovitch first set eyes on Hortense one summer in another city (the City, yours and mine, yours and theirs, its inhabitants, the City, in short, ours); she was walking down the street in the morning sunshine, and beneath her dress her body was bare of anything down under!

(The above sentence is admittedly a trifle ambiguous: it's impossible to say that there wasn't anything under Hortense's dress; she herself was there, if we grant that she bore her own body [and very well at that]; so there was something underneath: perhaps we should revise ourselves to read: "and beneath her dress she didn't bear the skimpiest fabric upon her upside down under": in all probability, this is what the expression "upside down" originally meant, afterward taking on a secondary connotation stemming from the disorder unfailingly sown in their wake by young women who dress likewise.)

This oversight, quite unintentional of course, had ultimately beneficial results, since the love of the Prince, whom Al. Vl. considered alone among human beings as his equal, had resulted from it; nevertheless Alexandre Vladimirovitch had retained the faintest hint of moral and (far worse perhaps) aesthetic reprobation.

"Plus," thought Hortense, "I know full well that he protects me from spies and assassins in the Enemy's hire—from mice, too. But isn't he around also to keep an eye on me?"

Just then a bell sounded. A split second beforehand, Alexandre Vladimirovitch had leaped down into the bathtub and, catching up the mother-of-pearl snail in his paw, he held it out to Hortense. It was the Prince on the phone.

Hearing the Prince's voice at the end of the nonline (it was a cordless phone), Hortense's breasts abruptly stood up as if uncovered without warning by a spring breeze slipping between two chemises. Until that moment they had rested so seemingly peaceful and satisfied upon her chest; but animated with a hope and a life all their own, they now moved upward, and in unison their homomorphic points hardened, while they swelled palpably in volume. Since this phenomenon occurred even before Hortense brought the earpiece to her ear, the impression created was that they (her breasts) had themselves been suddenly endowed with a sense of hearing. And it wasn't the Prince's voice alone that caused this, but the knowledge (shared by Hortense with her breasts) that the Prince's telephone was equipped with a full-screen video monitor in which she was visible from head to toe, in her moist, total nudity.

"Love in human females," thought Alexandre Vladimirovitch, witnessing the topological transformation, "love has strange effects. How far subtler with our females," he thought once again, "whose first hint of interest is shown only by the whiskers."

However, as the conversation progressed, a certain disenchantment became discernible in Hortense's breasts; soon, flatly disappointed, they returned to their initial, anerotic (as we'll call it) position. Perhaps (but we wouldn't swear to this) they sensed that the first chapter was drawing to a close.

Chapter 2

Why? Where? When? How? With What? With Whom?

Surrounded in total comfort, Hortense took all the time she needed to scrupulously scrub herself clean. As you'll have no trouble realizing on your own, a great deal of time inevitably went by. For, on the one hand, a 41-square-meter bathtub provides a rather vast track where, in Alexandre Vladimirovitch's absence, championship meets for cycling mice could be held during the unavoidably long time it takes to fill up; and on the other hand, the bathroom itself, covering about eighteen meters on each side, might well have inspired Hortense, either before her bath or afterward, to take a spin on some roller skates; all well and good. But where are we?

"On every subject," Father Risolnus explains in his fourteenth prelude entitled "Rhetortheorics or Rhetorhythmics," from his grand opus, the *Prolegomena rythymimorum*, "on every subject, an answer must be given—in the proper order, following the six modes of similarity, comparison, opposition of the deposition of the supposition, and knowledge of the circumstances—to six principal questions: **Why? Where? When? How? With what? With whom?**" Consequently:

Why? Because this is a novel, and the rules of the genre require it.

Where? In Poldevia, in the princely palace of Prince Gormanskoï, fiancé of the novel's heroine, Hortense.

When? Shortly before Christmas Day in the year of our Lord ——.

How? How what? I admit I don't understand the question.

With what? With what what? Perhaps it's a matter of finding out what Hortense soaps her caramel-colored thighs with; in this case, the answer is: with a red washcloth bearing the coat of arms of the Prince, her fiancé.

With whom? The most plausible answer must be: accompanied by Alexandre Vladimirovitch, Poldevian Cat Prince, companion and counsellor of Prince Gormanskoï, fiancé of Hortense, the novel's heroine.

The six questions are now answered, but we don't quite see how they enhance our understanding of the subject in any significant way. Rhetoric has failed us. So from now on we'll opt for the naked truth as she emerges from her bath like Hortense, unveiled, unadorned.

Once out of the tub, Hortense headed for the main room, accompanied by her bathrobe, which she casually tossed onto the sofa, and Alexandre Vladimirovitch; she snatched up the *Inferno Liber* guide to Poldevia and started skimming through it, and we along with her, as she searched for the information she needed.

"Poldevia," she read, "which some say was discovered in the Middle Ages by John de Mandeville, and others, by Marco Polo, or according to more recent theories, by ghastly Doctor Schutz, is located in an autochthonous, mountainous region of our terraqueous globe; populated, very likely since the Neolithic Age, by bandits and mustaches (often coexisting in the same body); its government is founded on the principaltariat principle, which experts in constitutional law term the **Poldevian Hexarchy**; in plain and simple language, this means that it is subject to six princes, the first of whom in the hierarchy is called the Premier Prince, the second, the Second Prince, and so on. As we go to press, the Presumed Premier Prince, recently back in our country, is Prince Gormanskoï. Prince G. . . ."

"Let's skip ahead," said Hortense to Alexandre Vladimirovitch.

This wasn't at all what she was looking for; she just wanted a map of the capital, Queneau'stown, so she could in due course find her way to the place where the Prince, during their telephone conversation in the first chapter, had planned for them to meet after she had stopped off to buy what he requested. Since we are following events from one main point of view, presently Hortense's—hence, and not without difficulty, reading over her shoulder—we no longer find it possible to continue with this nonetheless fascinating description of Poldevia. So despite our great wish to the contrary, we won't be able to expatiate upon its history and geography, the six religious creeds practiced by Poldevians, nor even upon the Poldevian language, so beautiful and so difficult, more difficult than Welsh, with its fifty-three consonants and eleven vowels, its six tones, and fourteen cases, nor upon the complexities of its political, economic, and social organization (we'll make up for this in a subsequent volume; and in these very pages, whenever the opportunity arises); even discussions about the weather are forbidden us; unless. . . .

After getting her bearings as best she could on the map (reproduced in part on page ix), Hortense raised her eyes to the window: the rain was coming down. Rain generally fell on the Poldevian principalities; over the radio every morning came the Universal Weather Report broadcast, subject to minute seasonal variations: "Long periods of rain will be interrupted by brief but violent downpours." And, as a matter of fact, an especially fierce downpour was horizontally lashing the panes; Hortense shuddered.

The predominance of rainfall can be easily explained: if it's not raining, it's a nice day; if it's a nice day, there are no clouds in the sky; if there are no clouds in the sky, it's blue; if it's blue, it's because of the ozone; but ozone is a treacherous element because escaping is its only goal; therefore, blue is the color of treason in Poldevian color symbolism; therefore, in ordinary weather, clouds fill the sky and, just as naturally and ordinarily, since clouds know how to do little else, from time to time and almost all the time, they release rain. Furthermore, rain is necessary for the well-being of snails which, as everybody knows, are the sacred animals of the Poldevians.

The rain was coming down.

Chapter 3

Following a Clue-strewn Course, Hortense Goes Christmas Shopping

Putting down the now useless *Inferno Liber* guide upon the pedestal table between the snuffbox and the small crystal carafe, Hortense stepped into the hallway and opened the closet. She picked out a very plain pair of red panties that barely fit over her tuft, riding very deep into her buttocks, a pair of black stockings, and garters with the Prince's coat of arms (you never know), a skirt that buttoned up the side, in a rather soft shade of red, a gray Poldevian cashmere pullover. She didn't put on a brasserie.

While she hesitated for a moment over what shoes to wear, memories of the past suddenly swept over her in the shadowy darkness of the hallway closet: in a lightninglike flashback Hortense relived the terrible, tragic events that, less than a few months before, had led her here to Poldevia: her abduction by the Prince's mortal foe, his diabolical double, his merciless nemesis; her last-second rescue from a fate worse than death; the berlin waiting in the darkness of night; the breathless flight toward the border in the carriage drawn by Carlotta's pony, Cyrandzoï. Her eyes clouded over, brimming with tears the way moisture mists a windowpane and blots out the view, the way a puff of breath hazes over a mirror and blots out a face: how far away it all was now!

And what had she become? A foreigner, holding a plain, temporary passport issued by the Hexarchy prefecture in acknowledgment of her status as the Presumed Premier Prince's fiancée, a foreigner greeted with suspicious glances at Court, who was a long way from everything and everybody: her parents, highly esteemed in the most select circles of the world of Haute Cold Cuts, her male and female friends, Laurie, Carlotta. . . . Her tears streamed more thickly. . . . And if the Prince . . .

Alexandre Vladimirovitch's fur moved gently against her leg: she could hear a soothing purr. She smiled, wiped her eyes (with a red, finely woven batiste handkerchief like the one Athos had in *The Three Musketeers,* but with the Prince's coat of arms) and walked back into her bedroom to get dressed.

Before meeting the Prince she had first to do some Christmas Eve shopping in the Palace neighborhood. Cyrandzoï was waiting with the grocery basket in front of the door. The six princely palaces stood on two sides of Place Sainte-Gudule, whose center had been occupied by a red derrick on top of a sandy hill ever since recently discovered oil reserves began flooding Poldevia with stupendous petropoldevodollar riches (which made the exchange rates for the Poldevian crown rocket beyond all expectations). She walked out through the metal gate and crossed the large park planted with oaks, baobabs, and age-old maples whose crowns were still dripping from the shower that had just ended; in Hortense's honor, the clouds held themselves despite having to go real bad.

To her right, flanked by the princes' chapel, jewel of baroque art, rose the majestic silhouette of Sainte-Gudule Cathedral, topped with its six domes like pomegranate-shaped pummels painted scarlet, purple, orange, blue, yellow, and green, respectively (the six basic colors of the spectrum according to Poldevian science) in honor of the six religions that called the cathedral their home. In the chapel garden, the snails joyously frolicked among the lettuce patches.

Turning off Avenue de l'Abbé-Migne, named after the famous compiler of the *Patrology* (a collection of writings by the Church Fathers), a gold-covered luxuriously bound edition of which could be found in a display case set in the wall adjoining the cathedral, she left the park and, accompanied by Alexandre

Vladimirovitch and Cyrandzoï the pony, stepped into the medieval maze of streets separating Sainte-Gudule from the Edbaun, the river dividing Queneau'stown like an emerald sword into two halves.

First she took Rue des Thousandmittens, where the abbot of Léthème, Father Risolnus, lived; at the corner, she turned left, then right, leaving another street on her left again, then a dead end, and, crossing Avenue des Raviolis, she went down Rue Gaston-Miron on her left; just as we suspected, she wound up at the Princes' Salmon Shop. Smoked salmon, either fresh or salt-water, is in fact the Poldevian national dish, and no Christmas can be celebrated without consuming a respectable amount of *Salmonidae.* Hortense chose some slices of Shetland in Cyrandzoï's honor, then paid with a Poldevian gold guinea. The salmon seller took the coin, weighed it in the palm of his hand, then examined it thoroughly to confirm its authenticity: hexagon-shaped, stamped with Marilyn Monroe's portrait, underneath which were the date and denomination: 1 Poldevian guinea. But that wasn't what the fishmonger was really looking for: each of the coin's six corners was numbered in sequence: the first, #1, was slightly scratched in such a way that the "1" looked like a small "i." Satisfied with the results, he put the coin into his cash register and smiled at Hortense, who received in addition and exchange four Poldevian farthings, which she placed carefully in her red velvet purse hanging around the pony's neck; then she was off.

(Warning: **each detail of this chapter must be observed with the strictest attention, for each is important in its own way and will not be brought up again.** It will be pointless, let's say thirty chapters into the novel—when for instance it will prove absolutely necessary to remember the amount Hortense spent to buy her Shetland smoked salmon for Christmas [and we do indeed mean "Shetland," not Norwegian, Batavian, or Cantalopian, and we do *now* indeed mean "Batavian" or "Cantalopian," not Finnish or Tasmanian], and the exact number and value of the coins changing hands—it will be too late, I say [or rather, "we" say] to complain about not understanding the reason behind a novelistic event *in toto* predetermined *precisely* by this narrative moment to which I draw, by way of example, and I do mean solely by way of example, precisely and presently, your attention [and this is no accident; nothing occurs by accident, not even accidents].)

(It has been pointed out to me that this novel is overrun with animals; we haven't even reached the end of Chapter 3 and already there is a sizeable number, either actually or potentially present: a cat, mice, a pony, snails, salmon, a mongoose, a koala [from California, who owed Carlotta a return visit following her own to San Diego. She spotted him up in his eucalyptus tree, chewing away at some eucalyptus leaves. "Hello," Carlotta said to him, "I've come from across the sea." The koala glanced at her with his beautiful koala eyes, wanted to answer, but his chin dropped to his chest and he fell asleep; on awakening, he decided to cross the ocean and return Carlotta's greeting, but he didn't make it in time for the novel—see *The Koala Murder Case* by G. P.], a hedgehog, a squirrel, etc.—for which I will be answerable. Exactly what my answer might be isn't too clear; consequently, I'll answer nothing.)

(Such an incredible number of animals, you say, but not a single dog! To that, my answer is simple: there haven't been any dogs in Poldevia since fleas were expelled in the fourteenth century, accused of spying for a foreign power [Japan, in all likelihood]; no more fleas, therefore, no more dogs.)

On her way back to the Palace, Hortense stopped off for a small *café-crème* at the Pony Shoe. Cyrandzoï ordered a pail of water and some fresh hay; Alexandre Vladimirovitch sat on the counter. Hortense set her packages on a chair; the rain had started coming down again. At the neighboring table, Father Risolnus had just noticed that his mug was empty.

"Get a move on, you miserable excuse for an innkeeper!" he shouted, "Another!"

15

Chapter 4

At the Pony Shoe Café

"Why 'another' and not 'the same'?" asked Father Risolnus's companion. The abbot became nonplussed for a moment; he had just spotted a radiant Poldevian girl enter the café, shivering in her rain-wet dress. To make her blush, he immediately blurted out an aside especially dear to his heart, and which he thought perfectly befitted his function as "abbot in etcetera partibus" of the order of Léthèmites.

(For the benefit of our reviewers, who are always waiting in ambush, ready to attack through the chink in our armor, we should explain that the sentence member "an aside" doesn't introduce a new character into this story, which has more than its share already [not to mention those who will be showing up in the near or distant future, a fact I'd like you to know about right now in order to avoid any misunderstandings; there are a lot of characters, and there are simultaneously more and less than meet the eye]. "An aside" is a simple enough lexical item, composed of two parts, "an" plus "aside," which Webster's will tell you comes from the theater world and which, still according to Webster's, is defined as "a remark addressed to someone offstage." The purpose for using it in the present context is to show, *subtly,* that Father Risolnus is pretending to address someone who is not on stage [i.e., not identified by the story], but in reality wishes to be overheard by the Poldevian girl in order to make her blush [a "chink in our armor" is also simple enough, a ready-made expression, whose definition, once again according to Webster's, I can give you—thanks to Carlotta, who phone-relayed both this and the other meaning—namely, "the gap between two pieces of armor." As for "ambush," my advice is to look it up for yourself, we've wasted enough time (I don't dare disturb Carlotta anymore, since I've just interrupted her twice in a row already while she was drawing a portrait of Ophelia for the characters of Carlotta and Ophelia: see further on, chapters 12 and 13, respectively)].)

"It's on me!" Father Risolnus had said (the variant: "Yum-yum," being saved for whenever he'd pass Poldevian girls on the street).

And, sure enough, the Poldevian girl blushed and her eyes met Hortense's, who assured her of her complete, undivided sympathy and support. Alexandre Vladimirovitch adopted a look of disgust in front of his bowl of warm, cinnamon-flavored milk.

But his companion's question checked Father Risolnus's delight as he watched shudders of embarrassment run across the girl's cheeks and other zones. He yanked out a few hairs from his chin, which he kept stubbly, and meditated upon the philosophic problem posed by the hard-and-fast synonymity of these two ostensibly contradictory expressions: "Waiter, another!" and "Waiter, the same!" The yellow-aproned waiter set down a pint of Valstar draft (imported beer in Poldevia) in front of Father Risolnus, who immediately ordered two espressos to buy himself some thinking time.

His morning beer buddy (who, for his part, stayed sober) was the famous philosopher Georges des Aquandbiens. A descendant of an ancient Etruscan family which had emigrated to Poldevia after the Revocation of the Edict of Naples, he taught at the University where—in a seminar taken by Hortense (who kept conscientious notes, which she forwarded to Laurie, Carlotta, and Ophelia [both before and during her adventures, she was a philosophy major])—he was currently lecturing on a text by Plato that has come down to us as the *Seventh Letter* (although in reality it's the sixth, as has been proven by Poldevian philologists). He prepared himself for class by using Laurie's answers to Hortense's letters and by eavesdropping on conversations in the Pony Shoe where he would come every morning for a chat with Father Risolnus. (This is no surprise to anyone familiar with the work habits of philosophers; already, on the shores of the Aegean . . .)

Father Risolnus had instantly forgotten the question, which left behind only a faint mnestic trace after his beer had disappeared inside him; nonetheless he sensed that it was philosophic in origin. And so when the waiter returned with the two espressos he used the opportunity to spark a discussion: the waiter (a handsome young man, who appreciated Hortense for all her true worth) picked the two red cups off his tray, setting down one in front of Father Risolnus, and the other in front of Georges des Aquandbiens.

"You've made a mistake," said Father Risolnus with the straightest of faces.

The waiter didn't think for a second.

"I'm sorry," he began, reaching to pick up both cups and switch them around.

Just then he froze, unable to understand how two cups of espresso could be mutually distinguished with reference to their destination (in the context of a customer's order, we mean). Father Risolnus let loose with one of his bawdy, scholar-abbot guffaws (which had taken him years to perfect).

"I've just tested out," he explained, "right before your eyes what I call the *Second Café Waiter's Syndrome.*"

All at once his interlocutor, the waiter, Hortense, Alexandre Vladimirovitch, Cyrandzoï, the Poldevian girl with her poise regained (her name? since you absolutely insist: Ariane), and a few other customers (including a snail) sprinkled around the café opened their ears wide. One and all were indeed familiar with the *Café Waiter's Syndrome,* but they (like you) were unaware of—until that precise minute, located just a little before the end of the fourth chapter of the novel entitled *Hortense in Exile* ("One can only wonder how any given passage of any given novel can refer to a 'precise minute'?"—a grouchy reviewer)—the existence of yet another, allegedly different, syndrome about café waiters whose most appropriate

18

name would be the "second syndrome."

"You are all familiar," Father Risolnus said, finishing off a new pint of Poldevian Valstar this time, which the waiter had brought, "with the *Café Waiter's Syndrome.* It goes like this: an order, flawlessly recorded in the brain of a trained member of that honorable profession, is instantly forgotten as soon as it reaches its destination. Professor Jeancheau, the famous Turkoman cognitivist, by shrewdly attaching some electrodes to the correct brain locations of a few specimens, which he subsequently autopsied, has determined beyond all doubt the emplacement in the left cerebral hemisphere of what henceforth can be called the mental organ of the café order, capable of carrying out those remarkable, instantaneous operations of memory storage and destorage. (Thus the professor was able to program a Turing machine which will any day now replace to everyone's benefit its far from perfect human counterpart—but that's another story.)"

Father Risolnus broke off.

"Waiter," he said, "the same; or rather," he added, struck by a sudden insight, "waiter, another. If I say: 'Waiter, the same'—now isn't that," he asked his interlocutor, "a philosophical problem of the first magnitude, a paradoxical synonymity? Where was I?"

"At the second syndrome," answered in chorus the Pony Shoe customers.

"Yes, yes, the second syndrome," Father Risolnus said distractedly.

"Here we go, he's forgotten again," thought Hortense.

But Father Risolnus hadn't forgotten.

"Let's suppose," he said, "that there's a rather large order— a glass of grenadine, another of rot gut, a Blue Lagoon, an orange juice, one lemon, and a lettuce leaf, for instance. By virtue of the first part of the first syndrome (the flawless storage in memory without which forgetting would have no meaning), the waiter will bring to the table the complete array of correct

19

items; but as soon as he starts handing them out to his customers, **he will necessarily make mistakes.** He will infallibly make mistakes, even if the order is no larger than two simple, and very different beverages. This syndrome—which I am proud to have been the first to formulate with complete scientific rigor—is still awaiting an explanation. The experiment that you've just witnessed, in which our friend here has played the role of unwitting guinea pig, delivers a striking confirmation of my hypothesis: between two identical, ordinary orders, in this instance two espressos, and faced with the customer's inevitable complaint, he immediately reacted as though he had made a mistake, as if he had known before the fact that he was going to make a mistake, as if he always made mistakes.

"Is 'the same,' " Father Risolnus then said, in a stunning flash of genius, "the same, or another? I ask you now."

A profound silence spread through the gloomy low-ceilinged room, dimly lit by the sunlight struggling through the clouds which had dropped almost to ground level in order to catch every last word of such a philosophically rich exchange.

Just then Hortense was seized by a terrible pang of anguish, whose meaning was at first a mystery. How could the *Second Café Waiter's Syndrome* produce such an effect upon her? She was not to remain for long in a state of such piercing uncertainty.

Chapter 5

The Foe

Three individuals had just entered the café. The first through the door was the trio's leader: although he was dressed like a prince, his outfit was **blue**, which announced to any experienced observer of Poldevian affairs the treason written in his heart; he was indeed a prince . . . alas! He was flanked by his confederates, two short-haired young men whose beauty intensified the intrinsic, inherent infamy of their tunics, also blue. They checked out the surroundings, hands clenched on the triggers of their water pistols (firearms are unknown in Poldevia; water-arms are especially popular: water pistols, water bombs, anti-hail cannons, plus some stink bombs once in a while).

Hortense recognized him at once; Alexandre Vladimirovitch's fur shuddered as if from an electric shock; his back bristled; the accursed Prince and his henchmen kept their distance, but the wretch's stare spiraled around Hortense's body, forcing her to turn her two arms into three hands for self-protection.

The Demon Prince was the personal foe of Prince Gormanskoï, Hortense's fiancé; from this point onward and for the rest of the book, we will refer to him by his nom de guerre: Augre. Likewise for Gormanskoï in this tale, whom sometimes we'll call Airt'n, which fits him at present for architectonic reasons. So then, Prince Augre, pursuing Prince Airt'n with fierce hatred, envious of the noble destiny of the man who was Presumed Premier Prince of Poldevia according to ancestral laws and traditions, attempted by every means within his power to take his place; and, far worse, to steal his fiancée, Hortense.

The two princes were as alike as two peas in a pod, but one was pure, the other poisonous. Only their trademark, a dot pattern tracing the line of the Poldevian spiral, stamped at birth on the left thigh of each of the princes (six in number), allowed them to be told apart when naked; and spotting this very mark at a crucial moment, Hortense was able to use her last ounce of strength to escape from the fate worse than death (but perfectly circumscribed in time and space) held in store for her by the lechery of the Prince, who had deviously passed himself off as the lover of our innocent and nearly ravished heroine.

But ever since then, the different moral natures of the two princes had been branded with a red-hot iron upon Hortense's soul; she no longer needed any material evidence to separate the wheat from the chaff. Even before spotting the Demon, she had felt his evil aura; what's more, the reactions of Alexandre Vladimirovitch and Cyrandzoï, ready to let loose with a kick, confirmed the matter in her mind. She might now have told him: "Even if I saw you naked from head to toe / Your bare flesh would not stop me from saying: 'No!' "

Removing his eyes from Hortense with seeming reluctance, Prince Augre went up to the counter and ordered three Fernet-Brancas.

While all this was going on, Gormanskoï (I mean, Prince Airt'n) arrived; the two princes looked each other up and down; Augre's face was stamped with an ironic grin which seemed to leave Airt'n indifferent; Hortense got up and with her fiancé walked into the street. The entire café heaved a sigh of relief.

Hortense and the Prince, accompanied by Cyrandzoï and Alexandre Vladimirovitch, ploughed their way as well as might be expected through the merry Poldevian mob moving in every direction at once now that the holidays were fast approaching. The traffic was heavy, but careful: don't go thinking it was because of all the cars. The stillness of the air was unbroken by any sounds from engines, unpolluted by any exhaust pipes; the recently discovered rich oil reserves were exclusively for exportation, and everybody got around by foot or bike; public and private means of transportation included wheelbarrows and double-decker buses drawn by small, sturdy, mountain ponies. Now and then the traffic along an avenue came to a complete halt so that a snail could take its own good time crossing; in Poldevia snails are off-limits to people, doing whatever they want and receiving deferential treatment. A sweet fragrance of pony dung wafted through the humid air.

So where were our heroes headed this pleasant winter morning—beautiful, gray, and rainy? Let's follow Gormanskoï's red cloak, Alexandre Vladimirovitch's soft, noble fur, Cyrandzoï's russet mane; let's follow the admiring and respectful gazes that accompany our beautiful heroine, Hortense. Striding firmly along, they made their way toward Place Queneleieff, on which stands the government palace, Eërlosni Castle.

Eërlosni Castle was a wooden structure in the past; having burned to the ground many times over and been rebuilt more beautifully every time, it was finally devoured by termites one hundred years earlier. The present-day structure is a renovated gasworks housing the courts, theater, museum, parliament, library, opera, school playground. . . . One wing provides apartment accommodations for the Reigning Prince. The building is surrounded by yellow pipework along which matching elevators for tourists ride up and down. It's very beautiful.

At the time our story opens (or rather, "opened," since we're already in Chapter 5), the Reigning Prince was married to Princess Gertrude, mother of the Presumed Premier Prince, but he wasn't the latter's father. Gormanskoï's father had been Reigning Prince; since he was dead, he had given up the throne, and Alcius, his brother, had taken his place both in the palace and Gertrude's heart—a fact that did not go entirely unnoticed by Hortense's fiancé.

The crowd was especially dense in front of the castle's main entrance, bustling with singers and curiosity-seekers, merchants

23

selling souvenir drek, doodads, and doughnuts; multicolored kites sailed skyward; pickpocketing sparrows relieved both merchants and bumpkins of their purses; choruses of orioles sang songs by Henry Purcell.

On their way in, our group crossed paths with a tall, bald, distinguished gentleman beaming with intelligence, whose face had been weathered by a stormy century. He was wearing a ripped pullover, a greenish Burberry raincoat, worn corduroy trousers, and espadrilles—a blue one on his left foot, a black on his right. In one hand he held a copy of the day's *Times,* in the other a red bag marked with "Big Shopper" (in English) from the top of which jutted a leek. He had a smile on his face.

They go inside.
A moment's pause.
The doors of the Palace's state room open at both ends.
Flourish. Enter in succession:
—from the right: Alcius, Reigning Prince of Poldevia;
Gertrude, his Princess; Poldevius, his Prime Minister; lords,
cops, and extras;
—from the left: Prince Airt'n, Presumed Premier Prince;
Hortense, his fiancée; Alexandre Vladimirovitch, Premier
Cat Prince; Cyrandzoï, Premier Pony Prince.

ALCIUS

Though yet of Airt'n our dear brother's death
The memory be green, and that it us befitted
To bear our hearts in grief, and our whole princedom
To be contracted in one brow of woe,
Yet so far hath discretion fought with nature
That we with wisest sorrow think on him
Together with remembrance of ourselves.
Therefore our sometime sister, now our princess,
Th'imperial jointress to this warlike state,

Have we, as 'twere with a defeated joy,
With an auspicious and a dropping eye,
With mirth in funeral and with dirge in marriage,
In equal scale weighing delight and dole,
Taken to wife. But now, my nephew Gormanskoï, and my son—

GORMANSKOï [*aside*]

A little more than nephew and less than "phew."

ALCIUS

How is it that the clouds still hang on you?

GERTRUDE

Good Gormi, cast thy nighted color off,
And let thine eye look like a friend on Poldevia.
Do not for ever with thy veilèd eyes
Seek for thy noble father in the dust.
Thou knows't 'tis common: all that lives must die,
Passing through nature to eternity.

GORMANSKOï

Ay, madam, it is common.

GERTRUDE

If it be,
Why seems it so particular with thee?

GORMANSKOï

Seems, madam? Nay, it is. I know not "seems."

25

(Flourish. Exeunt all but Airt'n-Gormanskoï, Alexandre Vladimirovitch, Cyrandzoï, and Hortense.)

Ah, that this too too sullied flesh would melt
Like butter and resolve itself into dew.
Or that the Everlasting had not fixed
His canon 'gainst self-slaughter. O God! God . . .
etc., etc.
                    Frailty, thy name is woman!
etc.
etc.
                                        No, no!

. . .

HORTENSE, ALEXANDRE VLADIMIROVITCH, CYRANDZOI
                    [*together*]

???

Chapter 6

Poldevians and Poldadamians

The meeting we've just witnessed between the Prince and his mother left Hortense (Hortense in particular, since the others must surely have had some inkling as to the meaning behind such behavior) in a mildly alarmed state of agitation and amazement. Ever since returning to Poldevia, her lover's odd conduct seemed both incomprehensible yet dictated by a logic that escaped her. "There's method in his madness," she thought, without feeling reassured. On the contrary. What's more, his affections had cooled whenever they found themselves alone, providing a new source of anxiety. He now seemed to be constantly concerned about the proper way to do things, and had stopped showering her with those expressions of impetuous ardor which she had grown so used to that she couldn't live without them. The only way she could make up for their absence was by resorting to memories and simulations that left her unfulfilled. (Have I made myself clear?) "What's going on?" she thought. "What's going on? Does he love me less?" she thought. "Does he love me less?" (She had an increasing tendency to stammer out her thoughts.) And who could she turn to for advice in this land of strangers? Of course there was Cyrandzoï—but he was so young!

As though nothing had happened, Gormanskoï (whom she absolutely refused to call by his new, unpronounceable name, Airt'n) joined her now, courteous, smiling. Somebody was heading toward them.

"Oh, no!" Hortense thought, "not *encore!*" (in her inner turmoil mixing English and French); for the newcomer, most certainly a prince, garbed in green, looked so much like Gormanskoï they couldn't be told apart. Their striking resemblance made her head spin: was the new man good, was he evil? Her instinct told her nothing, her love for the Prince transmitted no discriminant message: she kept looking at him, bewildered, flabbergasted.

"Darling, I'd like you to meet Prince Acrab'm; he's my brother, my ally, I love him like my alter ego. He's the One True Prince of Poldadamia, whose lands my enemy occupied during my absence. But all that's going to change, I can assure you!"

"*Ravi* to meet you, I'm sure," were the only words Hortense was able to mutter, again mixing French and English, a bit reassured but just as bewildered.

"All right," the Prince said, "let's go have a cup of tea now."

And they went to the tearoom Tea East Tea, on the banks of the pond, and sat at a table under the beeches on Avenue Parménidzoï. The pond is where the citizens of the capital most prefer to stroll: now an inland isle of water, it used to be a branch of the Edbaun River, cut off and left where it fell, almost with indifference: whether it engendered a pond or a not-pond didn't matter to the river, inhabited by nymphs, impatient to rejoin the sea. Small boats were traveling back and forth across the still, liquid sheet; children were launching their paper steamers; and dipping her hand into the almost lukewarm water, Hortense felt unsure about everything, herself included, in the same way that the pond did: "The pond is the pond; the not-pond is the not-pond; but could it be a not-pond and a pond both at the same time?" she muttered under the beeches.

The owner of the Tea East Tea had turned on the television; a singing group was wriggling around on the screen and everybody could hear the season's smash hit: "Are we not men? We are Pol-DEVO!"

Poldadamia, as ancient and mountainous as its neighboring

rival, Poldevia, has been waging an age-old and on-going battle for predominance in this region which history and geography "for once working hand in hand" have allotted both countries on this globe. The story of the complex, stormy relationship between these two peoples would take up (and does, in the *Encyclopaedia Poldevica,* to which we refer the reader) numerous volumes, and we'll confine ourselves here to a few sketchy but unavoidable facts.

According to folk etymology, which shouldn't be dismissed out of hand (for who can tell what grain of truth is buried in its pronouncements: for example, doesn't the derivation of the French word *haricot* [string bean] from *feve* [broad bean]: *faber* [Latin] turning into *favaricus-favaricotus-haricotus-haricot* demonstrate the profound culinary unity between "habada" [the *fevaie,* or broad bean family] from Navarre, and cassoulet from Toulouse, Carcassonne, or Castelnaudry?). "Poldevia" like "Poldadamia" is derived through sexual differentiation from "Polhumanity," which is in fact just a variation of "**PolPol.**" The suffix "**pol**" in demotic, archaic Poldevian (pre–Indo-European, closely related to the Greek word *polis:* "city"; living in cities is a distinctive trait of humankind), refers to "man," or more precisely "what is genuinely human in man" (the same suffix recurs in the opposition established by Poldevian critics between commercial art and genuine art, "Polart"). Hence, in the original Polpolis a distinction seemingly arose between which Pol belonged to Eve—Pol d'Eve (note the Gallic influence—*Translator's note*)—and which to Adam—Pol d'Adam—from which issued two different peoples. (In modern Poldevia, the man [or woman] in the street has moreover preserved this significant saying: "I don't know him from Pol d'Adam or Pol d'Eve.") Poldevians of today (like Poldadamians) still have a tendency to regard themselves as more human than other human beings insofar as they partici-pate in a common essence, the mythical *polpolis* ("the country of men and women who are the most manly and most womanly" is how we'll translate), which archeologists assure us has never existed.

This feeling of an ancient, deep-rooted identity between the two peoples, who speak each other's tongues (very closely related, it must be added), fostering a pro-reunification movement nearly as powerful as the current, irresistible force in our part of the world driving the inhabitants of the United Kingdom and the United States to become one again under the authority of the queen of England, is further consolidated by the problem of national borders. It is indeed no easy matter to tell where Poldevia begins and Poldadamia ends (and vice versa) at each point in each territory. The two hexarchies (both Poldadamians and Poldevians are ruled by six princes, who are moreover the same) have recently appointed a bipartisan commission to fix the frontiers once and for all so as to make it easier to find out how much would be lost in custom duties and capital flights if such duties and restrictions had existed between the two principalities. Such an estimate had been long demanded by economists and ministries of finance on both sides so that they could get their papers in order. The commission was made up of world-renowned scholars of topology with impeccable credentials (including among others, a Thomist, two Prigoginians, a Fractalist, a Benaboutist, and two Girardaucians). Their conclusion created a sensation: the border between Poldevia and Poldadamia forms in all probability a complete Peano curve, which means (we should clarify for our readers) that it runs unbroken (much to the despair of smugglers) and entirely fills the two territories; in other words, to look at things from a Poldevian point of view, which we adopt in this story, **the border is located everywhere, in every square inch of land, regardless how small.** Poldevia and Poldadamia cover the same mutually indiscernible territory.

Part Two

In Which a Twinship of Sorts Is Established with a Very Old Book

Chapter 7

Twins and Doubles

The Poldevian princes lead modest lives. Located in the very heart of the capital within a commoners' district dating from the Middle Ages, the hexarchy's six palaces don't stand out conspicuously from the homes of average citizens. Neither Poldevia nor Poldadamia, its rival sister nation, are poor; while their affluence is not ostentatious, the two countries could regardless be described as comfortably well-off. This explains why buildings, avenues, and parks here are all of a comfortable size; more comfortable than back home frankly. By way of comparison with our own City, if we station ourselves in the vicinity of the church whose namesake is the grand Poldevian cathedral, Sainte-Gudule, and if we sweep our eyes over a map—similar to the house and street relief map drawn to scale tacked up in Laurie, Carlotta, and Ophelia's kitchen (story characters whom we'll meet in Chapter 12; bear with me), we can spot a certain topographical similarity between this neighborhood and the one accommodating the princes. (The two map reproductions on pages viii and ix corroborate this.)

Prince Gormanskoï (Airt'n) possessed palace #1, on one of the corners of the square surrounding the park; immediately adjacent at a perpendicular angle was his foe's, Prince Augre's (at #4); Prince Acrab'm, brother, double, friend, and ally of Gormanskoï, was at #3, on the corner of Avenue de l'Abbé-Migne; the other palaces play no role in the present novel.

Airt'n had set aside for personal use just the third floor of his palace, renting out the others to honest, hardworking craftsmen; ever since getting back to Poldevia, he had been staying at his mother's, and Hortense had been living in his quarters, under the watchful eye of Alexandre Vladimirovitch.

After greeting Madame Echr'co, the Prince's janitress-in-chief, who handed over her mail, Hortense headed down the private avenue separated from the park by a solid-gold fence running along the foot of the palaces. Alexandre Vladimirovitch presented her with the small ruby-studded key he wore around his neck, and she opened the heavy entrance door; then she ascended the monumental red-carpeted staircase, on her way up patting the dear blond heads of the children from the second, fourth, and fifth floors who were waiting in respective ambush on the steps.

Hortense sat down on her bed and cradled her head in her hands. "How do you expect me," she said to Alexandre Vladimirovitch, "to keep my bearings?"

Alexandre Vladimirovitch had no expectations. He was seated in front of her upon a cushion on a chair, and he answered her telepathically, underscoring important thoughts with twitches of his whiskers.

"They're all the same; as soon as I learn to tell Airt'n from Augre a third one shows up who—and this is the final straw!—I'm not even supposed to avoid because he's a brother, friend, and ally."

Al. Vl. pointed out that Prince Acrab'm, whom he knew well and who was indeed a very honorable man, was not by any definition a "straw."

"Don't make fun of me," Hortense said, "you know perfectly well what I mean! 'My alter ego! My alter ego!' But all the same he doesn't want me to sleep with him! And it would be a good idea for him to sleep with me himself, I've had just about enough of this waiting-around business."

Alexandre Vladimirovitch had a disturbed look on his face: the direction which Hortense's thoughts were taking could not under any circumstances be approved; therefore he proceeded to make slight adjustments in his brain waves in order to lead

34

her back to the straight-and-narrow path of more appropriately speculative considerations.

"I've reached the point," she went on, "where I'm starting to see his doubles everywhere; for instance, that waiter a little while back at the Pony Shoe. Well now, I'm sure he's another." Al. Vl. neither confirmed nor denied this.

"All in all," she continued, "I've got to figure out what kind of movie I'm in."

"Movie?" Alex went.

"Well, movie script, story line, all that jazz, you know! Is it an original screenplay, or a rehash of Jekyll and Hyde, Mark Twain's twin, or the Cloven Viscount? I must admit that I'd find any one of these hypotheses extremely disagreeable."

Once more Alexandre Vladimirovitch showed his disapproval; but before answering, he'll translate Hortense's sibylline utterances for the reader: "Hortense is wondering (just letting her imagination run wild for the sheer fun of it, I hope) whether the miraculous multiplication of identities that seemingly characterizes Poldevian princes is genuine, or a sham; in other words, she's wondering whether there might not be just one prince who, a ventriloquist of appearances, is playing every role all by himself. And under the respective names of Jekyll and Hyde, Mark Twain, or the Calvinist Viscount, she is referring to three possible modes of such duplicity:

"—The first is Mark Twain's twin: it's common knowledge that Mark Twain had a twin brother; the twin's name was Luke, and he was such a perfectly identical match that even their mother wasn't able to tell her two sons apart; and one day, while taking their bath, one of the boys drowned; nobody ever discovered whether it was Mark or Luke." ("You've got that right," Hortense broke in, "except that you'd have to substitute quadruplets and call the other two John and Matthew! And what about the trademark? You haven't mentioned the trademark!" Alexandre Vladimirovitch refused to let himself be dragged into the debate: "Let's keep things simple; the situation's messy enough as it is.") "In this specific case, the double, the twin, is simply an illusion; there had always and at all times been only one person.

"—The second mode is Stevenson's novella: there's the good Dr. Jekyll and his evil incarnation, Mr. Hyde; they're like night and day, and indeed, they divide the weather between them: for the good Dr. Jekyll, sunshine; for the evil Hyde, night and fog.

"—The Viscount, last of all, was split in two by a cannonball during a battle; the good and bad half each went its own separate way; in this instance the halves aren't split by time, but by space.

"Take it from me, and you know this is the truth, not a single one of these hypotheses is admissible. The princes do indeed exist; moreover, Inspector Blognard, the finest detective in the world, discovered how to tell them apart, and **Blognard never makes mistakes!** If you consider only their physical properties, the six princes are indiscernible, and by virtue of the first half of Leibniz's Principle of Identity called the Identity of Indiscernibles (which I hope you're not confusing with its second twin half, the Principle of the Indiscernibility of Identical Bodies), they would therefore be identical. But at least their ethical properties separate them. A dreadful experience taught you how to tell apart Good Prince Airt'n, whom you love, from the Demon Prince, despicable Augre, who detests him and desires you, and whose one and only aim is to rape you and satisfy his insatiable lechery inside your sexy (I'm speaking for human ears) body.

"There's one thing you can be sure about: this distinction couldn't be more real. Take it from me, Alexandre Vladimirovitch. Of course, everything I've just said doesn't enable you to tell good from good, Airt'n from Acrab'm, a second distinguishing feature which in your case is necessary; but I'm convinced that you'll work it out. Let me tell you a little Poldevian fable (of which we have numerous versions, both Poldevian and Poldadamian); don't take it literally, it doesn't have *anything* to say

36

about the particular plight preoccupying you, it's just a fable, but fables have this habit of showing that sometimes unsuspected passageways exist to the reality behind appearances.

Fable of the Princess in Love with Twin Brothers

"Once upon a time there was a princess who was in love with a knight, but she didn't know which one: how is such a thing possible? Very simple: this knight had a twin brother, they were inseparable and mutually indiscernible; the princess knew that she didn't love both of them; she loved only one, but she didn't know which. Time and again she hesitated in her choice, but every effort she made to discern one from the other went wrong. So she decided to set—pardon the expression—her heart at rest. The way she decided to do this was by sleeping with each brother in turn. Which she did; and at once she was able to tell them apart: as a matter of fact, they were brother and sister."

"And which one did she love?" Hortense asked.

"The story doesn't say; all it says is that she was able to tell them apart."

"Indeed," Hortense said, "and a fat lot of good that does me!"

And she broke into song:

> I lived with her three years
> Until the day she suddenly said
> You look like Mom and Dad
> Horrors! She was my twin!
> And that's why we split, the lad-ee and me-ee . . .

"Alex," she said suddenly, breaking the silence, "do you think he still loves me?"

"Yes," the cat answered; and he leapt from his chair and went into the kitchen, thus signifying that the conversation had come to an end and that he was awaiting his salmon for lunch.

Chapter 8

A Very Disappointing Visit

Feeling in a little better spirits after her exchange of views with Alexandre Vladimirovitch and the fireworks of his feline dialectics, Hortense decided to get ready for the Prince's visit, which he had announced for teatime. She put on a nearly see-through blouse, a micro-miniskirt, left her feet bare, then she tried out several seating positions, each allowing a suggestive glimpse of her skimpy red panties, whose features we've already described. She knew that they were one of the Prince's favorite pair, which he had bought for her back during the time of his budding enthusiasm; and he had certainly not forgotten what promise the panties held, both before and behind.

Time passed; Sainte-Gudule tolled the hours (when I say hours, I mean quarter-hours, half-hours, three-quarter hours); Hortense had a grenadine; some misgivings about her outfit; changed clothes; changed again; finally decided on the same things she had picked out in the first place.

Meanwhile teatime approached; then arrived.

Alexandre Vladimirovitch, once fed, had a short purr, followed by a short nap just to show what it meant to lead a comfortable life with your conscience at peace and a perfectly suspended judgment. Afterward, he quietly slipped off for a little romantic rendezvous of his own in Sainte-Gudule Park.

Six to five, five to, four to, three to.

Two to five.

One to five.

Fifty-nine seconds to five, fifty-eight . . ., fifty-three.

. . . thirty-five . . ., eighteen . . ., fourteen, eleven, nine, six, five, three, two, one.

The intercom rang.

Hortense: "Who's there?"

The Prince: "Prince Gormanskoï, Madame."

Hortense: "Second door on the right."

After saying the words "Second door on the right" and pressing the buzzer to admit him, Hortense had a flash of intuition that nothing was happening according to her expectations. She felt as though she were being swept up in spite of herself into a sequence of events robbing her of any willpower, in which her speech and gestures were dictated from a very distant point in time and space outside the action. She was simultaneously watching a scene in which she was forced to play an incomprehensible role.

She and the Prince were in the largest room of the apartment. Standing face to face, Hortense had her back to the windows; the Prince, looking out through them. He talked to her as though he couldn't see her, or saw some other invisible presence standing just off to her side. And she answered likewise, using somebody else's words, ones not of her choosing but which she uttered all the same as though compelled. Once in a while, infrequently, with an enormous burst of willpower, she managed to fit a few of her own words into the flood of foreign talk coming out of her mouth, but she got the definite feeling that he didn't really hear them, and so what she said was in vain. Yet, alas, she herself could make out what the Prince was saying, words she didn't want to hear, flooding her with great sorrow.

G: "Nymph, in thy orisons
Be all my sins remembered."

H: "Good my lord,
How does your honor for this many a day?"

G: "I humbly thank you, well, well, well."

H: "My lord, I have remembrances of yours
That I have longèd to re-deliver . . ."

G: "No, not I

I never gave you aught."

H: "My honored lord, you know right well you did,
And with them words of so sweet breath composed
As made the things more rich. Their perfume lost,
Take these again; from my mouth, from . . .
Rich gifts wax poor when givers prove unkind.
There, my lord."

G: "Ha, ha! Are you honest?"

H: "My Gorm . . . my lord!"

G: "Are you fair?"

H: "What do you . . . what means your lordship?"

G: "That if you be honest and fair, your honesty should admit no discourse to your beauty."

H: "Could beauty, my lord, have better commerce than with honesty?"

G: "Ay, truly; for the power of beauty will sooner transform honesty from what it is to a bawd than the force of honesty can translate beauty into his likeness. . . . I did love you once."

H: "Indeed, my lord, you made me believe so."

G: "You should not have believed me. . . . Get thee to a nunnery; go, and quickly too. Farewell!" [*Exit*]

HORTENSE: "O, woe is me!"

Chapter 9

The RGBLP

After crying most of the night long, after being comforted and lulled to sleep in the early morning by her "pet-à-pet" with Alexandre Vladimirovitch; after having her tea with scones, baps (the real, old-fashioned, very hard kind like they don't make in Edinburgh anymore, which Cyrandzoï bought at the Groichanskoï Bakery), and muffins, smothered in heavy double cream from Cornwall—Hortense decided to go to the library and do some thinking. Only in libraries could she have a good think. She had met the Prince in a library. And, at any rate, she wanted to give Poldevia's new library a try; in memory of the good old days (whose violins and monotonous languor brought tears to her eyes) the Prince had arranged for her to have a permanent user's card. She would take advantage of this opportunity to check out a certain textual hypothesis which she had just elaborated during her bout of insomnia; in addition, she'd write a letter to Laurie, Carlotta, and Ophelia, with a P.S. from Alexandre Vladimirovitch on the one hand, and from Cyrandzoï on the other, especially for Carlotta (whose acquaintance [or reacquaintance, depending on what you've read] you'll be making in less than three chapters, along with Laurie and Ophelia, and that's a promise).

The new Poldevian library was called the **RGBLP,** i.e., the **Real Great Big Library of Poldevia** (for Poldevians) or the **Real Great Big Library of Poldadamia** (for Poldadamians). When it was first conceived, long discussions were held about the name: some wanted to call it just the **Real Great Big Library of Poldevia** (these were the Poldevian fundamentalists);

others wanted to limit the name to the **Real Great Big Library of Poldadamia** (these were the Poldadamian fundamentalists); still others (Poldevians), in a spirit of reconciliation, proposed the **RGBLPP (Real Great Big Library of Poldevia and Poldadamia)**; but the debate raged even worse than before, because some (Poldadamians especially) pointed out that there was then no good reason for referring to it as the **Real Great Big Library of Poldevia and Poldadamia** instead of the **Real Great Big Library of Poldadamia and Poldevia;** at which point, a faction of the reconciliation party, immediately christened "hyper-reconciliators," rallied to the following solution: the name of the library would be **RGBL (PP and PP) (Real Great Big Library of Poldevia and Poldadamia, and Real Great Big Library of Poldadamia and Poldevia)**. But you can clearly see that despite everything it was still a burning issue. The result was that the governments of both states finally agreed on the solution mentioned in the beginning of this paragraph. Both names were inscribed into the pediments of each of the six towers comprising the library, and their respective positions shifted every day according to the results of a lottery drawing entrusted to the innocent hands of the chaste maidens of Sainte-Gudule, dressed in the violet befitting the occasion.

In front of the monumental entrance—an arch of triumph engraved in gold with "ISBN"—the director of the RGBLP, Baron LeDroit-Pénurie, was blowing on the thermometer to raise the temperature, which had decided to drop as Christmas neared. Baron LeDroit-Pénurie had been the director of the former library which, for reasons unknown, after being the honor and glory of the principalities for centuries, suddenly started to malfunction on a massive scale. Extensive investigations were conducted into the causes behind these catastrophes, but without result. The wildest hypotheses were proposed: shortages of storeroom space, or of staff; inadequate salaries; cramped, shoddy work areas. . . . In the end, Baron LeDroit himself had discovered the culprit: a foreign book by a certain

J****** R******, a novel entitled *O** B******** H*******, recently acquired by the library, and in which **libraries were made fun of!** Of course, this grating satire devoid of a single drop of humor in all apparent likelihood (once you strip away the trappings behind which the author had intended to disguise his wrongdoing) takes aim at a *different* library, the B*********** N******** of P****; but, in reality, all libraries were targeted, portrayed as monsters, and most of all, the *Big Poldevian Library* of which he, Baron LeDroit-Pénurie, was the director. His library was ridiculed, called sadistic and incompetent; stricken by such injustice, unable to react in the face of so much dishonesty, it was little wonder that the library sank into depression. At the baron's request, the authorities decided to pull the offending book from bookstores and, above all, expel it from the library; but, alas, the hard fact had to be faced: somebody had filed it under the wrong classification number; the criminal copy could not be found!

The Reigning Co-Princes then made the following decision: a new library had to be constructed.

They would take advantage of the opportunity to build a postmodern building, equipped with all the latest innovations of present-day science and technology that would make Poldevia and Poldadamia envied the world over. The necessary funds were authorized by Parliament, on the princes' orders; then unfrozen; after which construction began.

One problem remained: what would become of the *former library* in the future, and its numerous volumes, the treasures of knowledge it held? Some gullible souls imagined that, since the RGBLP was new, it could make a new beginning from scratch and build up its collection either by acquiring every forthcoming publication (or as many as possible), or—moving toward that other future, i.e., the past—by duplicating, reproducing, or storehousing (thanks to the wonders of technology) works contained in the former library. This modest proposal met with resolute, effective, and vehement opposition: every Poldevian

43

and Poldadamian researcher signed a petition railing against the anti-epistemological "break" in knowledge that would result from any such decision; furthermore, for many years to come, so they said, they would have to change places in order to have access to the old collection, whereas it would be ever so much more pleasant to have everything within arm's reach in the new library. But once again, it was Baron LeDroit-Pénurie who came up with the irrefutable argument: if the present library were left in good working order, the criminal text in its collection, the one responsible for its paralysis, would remain where it was, since it was impossible to place it in custody. Far from having on their hands some venerable old library with a touching old reading room to which so many backward-looking souls were attached, they would be saddled with some good-for-(practically)-nothing, chronically depressed old wreck. By contrast, a transfer, by providing the uphoped-for opportunity of an exhaustive inventory, would permit them to flush out the pernicious ferret, the perfidious fox, the greedy badger which had sneaked into the chicken coop of books—and they would be rid of it once and for all.

The decision for a total transfer was therefore made and carried out; a few disgruntled people—having observed that if the new towers were flooded with such a vast amount of books they would most likely be all full, despite their imposing dimensions, before they even went into operation—were informed that, naturally, not every single one of these old documents (plainly useless in the majority) were going to be put into such a brand-new, clean, resplendent, and expensive place. The physicists proposed destroying all useless books; when asked how they would choose, it came out that nearly all of them considered as entirely worthless any book or article that had not been reviewed within the past three years in *Physical Review*. Once this modern and progressive solution was ruled out (since it was frowned on by the other great libraries of the world), an agreement was made that nothing whatsoever would be destroyed, but instead every work without a useful purpose would be exiled to silos located in a mountainous region from which they could be recalled, given some demonstrated extraordinary need, within forty-eight hours.

"But," asked the same fainthearted grouches, "how would these 'works without a useful purpose' be selected?" "It's very simple," came the answer, "they'll consist of all those which, in the former library, were never, or very rarely, requested by a reader."

And so that's how the system functioned. All those people who, through some mental aberration unimaginable in our day and age, had undertaken research on certain books whose contents, precisely because they hadn't been read, were a mystery, understood after a few months of these operating procedures the utter triviality of their obsolete notions. The majority gave up: a few became financial analysts.

Chapter 10

The RGBLP (continued)
and a Strange Apparition

The library's inner entrance, located after the outer ramparts where Hortense presented herself along with her membership card and diplomatic passport, fulfilled a twin function:

1. It separated readers from nonreaders, as in most libraries (with this difference, that it was a good idea for a reader to have two cards, both a Poldevian and a Poldadamian one, because on certain days the library was Poldevian and those who only had cards to the other library were turned away, and viceroy's virgins [*note:* a Poldevian expression for "vice versa"]).

2. It served as a frontier post between the two countries; since every point within the territory was also situated along the border and thus a point of passage from Poldevia into Poldadamia as well as, *and in the same direction* (which exceeds the capabilities of most countries), reciprocally from Poldadamia into Poldevia, a decision was made to establish at this exact spot a symbolic frontier crossing (and what could be more highly symbolic than a library entrance?) for passport and customs inspections. Soldiers from both countries kept round-the-clock guard. They checked IDs and membership cards, which explains why Hortense brought along her passport.

There was a genuine mountain frontier-post setting painted in trompe l'oeil with a Thomas Mannish feel, and the heavily armed guards, in fur caps and bundled in their uniforms, used their binoculars to scrutinize newcomers at the far end of the avenue leading in from the ramparts.

That morning.
Enter Claudio B. and Francisco C., sentinels.

CLAUDIO B.: "Who's there?"
FRANCISCO C.: "Nay, answer me. Stand and unfold yourself."
    CLAUDIO B.: "Long live the Reigning Prince!"
    FRANCISCO C.: "Claudio?"
    B.   "He."
    F.: "You come most carefully upon your hour."
    B.: " 'Tis now struck twelve [*commentator's note:* symbolic hour]. Get thee to bed, Francisco."
    F.: "For this relief much thanks. 'Tis bitter cold,
        And I am sick at heart."
    B.: "Have you had quiet guard?"
    F.: "Not a mouse stirring, nor a cat."
    B.: "Well, good night." (*To Hortense, who shows her card and passport.*) "Good-day to you, mademoiselle."
Exit Francisco.
Enter Marcellus B. and Prince Acrab'm.
MARCELLUS B.: "Holla! Claudio B."
    CLAUDIO B.:   "Say
   What, is Prince Acrab'm here?"
MARCELLUS B.: "A piece of him."
    CLAUDIO B.: "Welcome, Marcellus B. Welcome, Prince Acrab'm."
    M.: "What, has this thing appeared again tonight?"
    C.: "I have seen nothing."
    M.: "The Prince says 'tis but our fantasy, . . .
        Therefore I have entreated him along
        With us to watch the minutes of this night
        That, if again this apparition come,
        He may approve our eyes and speak to it."
THE PRINCE: "Tush, tush, 'twill not appear."
Enter Ghost.

THE PRINCE: "In the same figure, like the Reigning Prince that's dead
Father of my brother and friend Gormanskoï
Called Airt'n, Premier Presumed Prince,
Fiancé and lover of Hortense.
(*To the ghost.*) Speak, speak! By heaven I charge thee, speak!"
Exit Ghost.

Still shaken by this weird, Gothic apparition, Hortense went over to the first tower, the red one, to begin her research. Each tower had its own individual color (the second tower was violet, the third orange . . .). The transparent tinted glass towers were each thirty-seven stories high (at present, because later on floors would be added as the need arose), which you ascended either by the stairs or elevators running along the walls. Each reader sat in his small personal cubicle, with his documents, reading and recording equipment, word processors, telephones, videophones, printers, pencils, diskettes, and once in a while, even an occasional book; and the library visitors, chiefly the countless, interchangeable tourists, watched them as they passed along, pressing up against the windows, making funny faces, taking pictures and trying to catch their attention and distract them from their readerly tasks; but in vain, because the readers couldn't see them.

One of these small cages was occupied by a tall, bald man, extremely intelligent, cultivated, and distinguished, whose face had been weathered by a stormy century; he was wearing a ripped pullover, a greenish Burberry raincoat, worn corduroy trousers, and espadrilles—a blue one on his left foot, a black on his right; on his desk he had placed a copy of the *Times;* at his feet was visible a red shopping bag marked with "Big Shopper" (in English), from the top of which jutted a leek. He had a smile on his face. He was smiling and reading *Gone with the Wind.* In reality, he wasn't reading, he simply had the book open in front of him, and he was listening to a parrot who was reciting the text, page by page, chapter by chapter. This was a new service recently offered to the readers of the RGBLP: a book was recorded by actors, then read before specially trained parrots who learned it effortlessly by heart: a reader just needed to send out the appropriate order slip and at once the parrot raced to the spot, ready to recite. On this reader's desk, near the *Times* spread open to the "Court Circular" page which reports on the royal family's whereabouts, snatches of an unfinished letter fell within our reading view: ". . . it's about a *gnomonologue,* a literary genre I plan to launch on this occasion; it possesses great philosophic, poetic, and esoteric depth; I've just begun it; it goes something like: 'To be being or not being having the whole while been or not been, that's the nagging question, etc.' "

Hortense was headed for the red tower where the books had been divided up along the rational principles of the hyper-libraries whose classification system was ingeniously invented ages ago by a Poldevian Renaissance author named Paolo de Brafforte, a disciple of Leonardo of Pisa. His system treats what is technically called "Ordered Libraries"; here we can give only a brief survey of his grandiose conception, which amazingly remains to be adopted the whole world over (if the world can be called "whole," that is; it strikes us as rather fractional):

—In one section the works were arranged *numerically:* first, those containing the number one in their title; next, those containing the number two; then three (*The Three Musketeers,* for example); four (*The Sign of the Four* by Arthur Conan Doyle); five (*Five Weeks in a Balloon*); twenty (*Twenty Years Later*)—and so on, all the way to the power of fourteen (*100,000,000,000 Poems* by Raymond Queneau).

—In another section, books had been collected according to *colors* (*The Red and the Black, Old Yeller, Green Gabardine, Orange Virus*).

—In still other locations, there were those books containing (once again in the title) the words *isosceles,* as well as *sparrow owl, whatsoever, hierarchy, (I) would argue...* (these words were devised by Marcellus B.).

An unlimited number of varieties can be devised, and the libraries of the RGBLP were constantly discovering new ones which they experimented with immediately to the supreme delight and benefit of their readers.

Another cataloguing principle was "portmanteau" words, devised by a librarian from the British Museum, Reverend Dodgson (and sometimes referred to, for mysterious reasons, as "suitcase" words).

—Thus, there was "suitcase geography," where you could discover "Lithuanicaragua," "Perumania," "Nebraskatchewan," and other obscure but henceforth indispensable cultural entities.

—"Suitcase authors" allowed for daring semantic comparisons and numerous critical discoveries: what could be more natural than a catalog dedicated to the works of Henry James Joyce, Tolstoyevski, and Shakespirandello!

As a matter of fact, Hortense was pouring over the works of the latter, and before long she confirmed what she, like we, had suspected; she felt far from relieved for all of that; quite the contrary!

(The passage that follows has been cut and mutilated by the Author, but [partially] restored at Hortense's request.)

She lingered where she was a while; the place wasn't familiar like the City library back home where she had her set ways, and with which she had at one period managed (when given time enough to read and think) to establish an almost affectionate relationship; yet it was still a library. And Hortense liked libraries. Life went by at a calmer and more peaceful pace here, free of passion's joys certainly, but also of its storms. You were even able to do some thinking and learning. She raised her eyes from the book she had come to consult, reflecting: "What if I read something that I find personally interesting, and not the novel of my adventures?" She glanced around. "They" didn't seem to notice her. A sentence flashed upon her monitor: "Do you wish to read another work?" She . . .

From one of neighboring seats in the reading room of the Ordered Libraries, Father Risolnus waved to her; he was jumping with joy because he had just discovered a crucial argument concerning the essential nature of rhythm in the titanic struggle that pitted him against his lifelong theoretical opponent, Louis Macaniche. The latter, in a recent article, had accused him of *"evacuating both the subject and history."* However, Father had just proven that rhythm is inexorably and rigorously deduced from the very existence of protons, the solid elementary building blocks that comprise our sensible world. "When we slam our faces into a wall," he confided to Hortense, "it's because of protons." But the calculable life span of a proton is longer than the universe's itself, which is to say that protons, and rhythm along with them, are for all practical purposes eternal. "So there," Father Risolnus said, "take that! 'The subject and history'! Don't they look like fools! Phooey!" and on his monitor he called up in an amber 18-point Geneva relief font (savagely censored by the Publisher) the conclusion of his article for the *Review of Poldevian Poldevian Metaphysics and Morality* (not to be confused with the *Review of Poldevian Poldadamian Metaphysics and Morality,* entirely devoted to Macanichian ideas).

"ONLY ONE UNIVERSAL CONSTANT EXISTS: RHYTHM!

"MATTER, SPACE AND TIME BEING INDISSOCIABLE AND CO-PRESENT, IN OTHER WORDS TOTALLY REAL OVER INFINITESIMAL PERIODS, RHYTHM IS THE ESSENCE-EXISTENCE OF EVERYTHING FOUNDED ON NOTHINGNESS. THE RHYTHMIC PULSATION OF THE VOID IS THEREFORE THE FUNDAMENTAL GNOSEOLOGICAL CATEGORY, THAT IS TO SAY GOD. THIS RESULTS IN CORRECT THEOLOGY."

A little while later over in the Pony Shoe he read the above words to Hortense, Al. Vl., Cyrandzoï, little blush-cheeked

51

Ariane, and the waiter, a handsome young man; in front of a fresh, very cold pint of beer, he finished up with a hymn that one of his friends had composed in honor of Louis Macaniche:

Hymnus Rythmi

(do si la sol   sol la la la la la sol   fa mi re   si la sol la   sol fa
mi sol do   do do do do sol do sol do re mi do   re re re re re re re
do re mi re do   mi do: *old Poldevian folk tune*)
1 Notzo fa   rin the town of Touarry
la la la   la la la la la la la la la
Notzo fa   rin the town of Touarry
la la la la la la la   la la la la la   la la
    2 Less it zout toward Montwarry
la la la   la la la la la la la la la
    Less it zout [etc.]
    3 Or elz maybe   in Ferte below Jouarry
la la la   la la la la la la la la la
    4 The poewuhtishians held their consistouarry
la la la   la la la la la la la la la
    5 Father Risolnus read from his gramaryerry
la˙la la   la la la la la la la la la
    6 About Rhythmoum an imposing treatisererry
la la la   la la la la la la la la la
    7 Every poewuhtishian   got the pictuarry
la la la   la la la la la la la la la
    8 Wen Macaniche   took out his slingshottery
la la la   la la la la la la la la la
    9 "U revacuatin the Subjik and Histouarry!"
la la la   la la la la la la la la la
    10 Ever since   after downin on the contrarry
la la la   la la la la la la la la la
    11 A Guinness   no blacker can beer ever be-erry
la la la   la la la la la la la la la
    12 Sing we all   on our way to the pissouarry
la la la   la la la la la la la la la

13 "Let zevacuate   the Subjik and Histouarry!"
la la la   la la la la la la la la la
    "Let zevacuate the Subjik and Histouarry!"
la la la la la la la   la la la la la   la la!!!

Chapter 11

The Letter to Laurie, Carlotta, and Ophelia

Hortense would have felt all the more remarkably insecure had she been able to witness the meeting between Prince Gormanskoi and the ghost the evening of that very day, along with those subsequent frightening revelations; all the more insecure since, in light of what she had read (or rather, re-read) that very morning in the library, she would have been pretty much capable of describing what the meeting was about, which was the situation's least disturbing angle; and so she dashed off a letter to Laurie:

QUENEAU'STOWN, POLDEVIA,
PALACE OF PRINCE GORMANSKOI
THIS SUNDAY, DECEMBER —, 19—

Dear Laurie, Dear Carlotta, Dear Ophelia: In order to explain what's happening to me, it would probably be best if I copy out the tale of my adventures such as it appears in the book dedicated to them and now being written, *Hortense in Exile;* I've underlined and numbered a few especially important passages in case you don't have time to read everything:

from Part One

from Chapter 1
1 Just then a bell sounded. A split second beforehand, Alexandre Vladimirovitch had leaped down into the bathtub and, catching up the mother-of-pearl snail in his paw, he held it out to Hortense. It was the Prince on the phone.

2 Hearing the Prince's voice at the end of the nonline (it was a cordless phone) Hortense's breasts abruptly stood up as if uncovered without warning by a spring breeze slipping between two chemises.

3 However, as the conversation progressed, a certain disenchantment became discernible in Hortense's breasts; soon, flatly disappointed, they returned to their initial, anerotic (as we'll call it) position.

from Chapter 2
4 Blue is the color of treason in Poldevian color symbolism; therefore, in ordinary weather, clouds fill the sky.

from Chapter 3
5 Hortense stepped into the hallway and opened the closet. She picked out a very plain pair of red panties that barely fit over her tuft, riding very deep into her buttocks, a pair of black stockings, and garters with the Prince's coat of arms (you never know), a skirt that buttoned up the side, in a rather soft shade of red, a gray Poldevian cashmere pullover. She didn't put on a brasserie.

6 Hortense chose some slices of Shetland in Cyrandzoï's honor, then paid with a Poldevian gold guinea. The salmon seller took the coin, weighed it in the palm of his hand, then examined it thoroughly to confirm its authenticity: hexagon-shaped, stamped with Marilyn Monroe's portrait, underneath which were the date and denomination: 1 Poldevian guinea. But that wasn't what the fishmonger was really looking for; each of the coin's six corners was numbered in sequence: the first, #1, was slightly scratched in such a way that the "1" looked like a small "i."

from Chapter 4
7 "Is 'the same,' " Father Risolnus then said, in a stunning flash of genius, "the same, or another? I ask you now."

from Chapter 5
8 Striding firmly along they made their way toward Place Quenelieff, on which stands the government palace, Eërlosni Castle.

9 *The doors of the Palace's state room open at both ends.*

Flourish. Enter in succession:
—from the right: Alcius, Reigning Prince of Poldevia; Gertrude,
his Princess; Poldevius, his Prime Minister; lords, cops, and extras.
—from the left: Prince Airt'n, Presumed Premier Prince; Hortense,
his fiancée; Alexandre Vladimirovitch, Premier Cat Prince;
Cyrandzoï, Premier Pony Prince.

ALCIUS

Though yet of Airt'n our dear brother's death
The memory be green, and that it us befitted
To bear our hearts in grief, and our whole princedom. . . .

from Chapter 6
10 The newcomer, most certainly a prince, garbed in green, looked
so much like Gormanskoï they couldn't be told apart. Their striking
resemblance made her head spin: was the new man good, was he evil?
Her instinct told her nothing, her love for the Prince transmitted no
discriminant message; she kept looking at him, bewildered, flabbergasted.

"Darling, I'd like you to meet Prince Acrab'm; he's my brother, my
ally, I love him like my alter ego."

from Part Two

from Chapter 7
11 "A dreadful experience taught you how to tell apart Good
Prince Airt'n, whom you love, from the Demon Prince, despicable
Augre, who detests him and desires you, and whose one and only aim
is to rape you and satisfy his insatiable lechery inside your sexy (I'm
speaking for human ears) body. There's one thing you can be sure
about: this distinction couldn't be more real. Take it from me,
Alexandre Vladimirovitch. Of course, everything I've said doesn't
enable you to tell good from good, Airt'n from Acrab'm, a second
distinguishing feature which in your case is necessary; but I'm convinced that you'll work it out."

from Chapter 8
12 G.: "You should not have believed me. . . . Get thee to a
nunnery; go, and quickly too. Farewell!" [*Exit*]

from Chapter 10

13 *Enter Ghost.*

THE PRINCE: "In the same figure, like the Reigning Price that's dead
   Father of my brother and friend Gormanskoï
   Called Airt'n, Premier Presumed Prince,
   Fiancé and lover of Hortense
(*To the ghost.*) Speak, Speak! By heaven I charge thee, speak!
Exit Ghost.

14 What could be more natural than a catalog dedicated to the works of Henry James Joyce, of Tolstoyevski, and Shakespirandello! As a matter of fact, Hortense was pouring over the works of the latter, and before long she confirmed what she, like we, had suspected; she felt far from relieved for all of that; quite the contrary!

from Chapter 11

15 Hortense would have felt all the more remarkably insecure had she been able to witness the meeting between Prince Gormanskoï and the ghost the evening of that very day, along with those subsequent frightening revelations.

There, I think that's the heart of the matter; my darlings, these excerpts will give you a clear idea of the very serious situation I find myself in; even more serious than you might think after reading the preceding chapters: this morning when I woke up, I was surprised to catch myself singing a song I didn't know and whose lyrics I didn't understand; here's how it begins:

> And will 'a not come again? [*repeat*]
> No, no, he is dead;
> Go to thy deathbed
> . . . .

Am I going mad?

Take my word, **there's something rotten in the Principalities of Poldevia.**

Come with your help, I beseech you.

Sincerely,
Hortense

P.S. (don't show this to the Author; I wrote it in invisible ink and it will show up only on the galleys; he won't even notice).

Printer's note: this postscript did indeed show up just after the manuscript was handed over and it's likely that it wasn't read by the persons to whom it was sent.

I don't need you just to clear up the mysteries threatening me; but plain and simply because I miss you; I don't have anybody to talk to; just a cat which isn't even mine, since he's a Prince. I feel lonely and at the same time like some punching bag, that is, I don't feel alone enough: there is no time set aside in a punching bag's schedule for meditation; I'm caught right in the thick of plots beyond my control and I'm helpless; maybe you can drop the Author a few lines; he doesn't seem to realize that the mechanics of Eros are cutting me off from the world and the dynamics of love are wearing me out.

Chapter 12

Meanwhile, Back in the City,
Not Far from Sainte-Gudule

Meanwhile, back home in the City, Christmas was also drawing near despite the difference in time zones. Laurie and Carlotta were in the kitchen of their apartment in building "X," 53 Rue des Citoyens, the entrance of which opened on Square des Grands-Edredons adjoining Sainte-Gudule. They were preparing their shopping list for Christmas dinner on recycled paper bought in the same store where you can sign a petition to save the badgers and where volunteers are ready round-the-clock to give refuge to whales seeking political asylum. From her position atop the cabinet above the refrigerator Ophelia checked that they weren't forgetting about her on their list of those prime, absolutely essential items marked with a *** in the margin. The top of the cabinet above the refrigerator can be reached by leaping on Laurie's armchair, from there onto the refrigerator, from there onto the upper edge of the kitchen door, then from the kitchen door to the top of the cabinet. This strategic position allows Ophelia:

—to keep an eye on newcomers through the opening kitchen door;

—to check that Laurie and Carlotta haven't omitted the absolutely essential items from their shopping list (Christmas or no Christmas), i.e., cans of cat food;

—to try out new cat postures, both from an aesthetic and a moral point of view, as well as to adjust and perfect the old ones.

But who is Ophelia? Who are Laurie and Carlotta?

Laurie and Carlotta were redheads (they still are, but the

requirements of narration compel verb forms to be used in the appropriate narrative tenses; we know, certainly, that Laurie and Carlotta, having been redheads in the period preceding the start of the narrative, stand an excellent chance of being redheads during the events narratively reported by the narrative, and consequently and in all likelihood will remain so at the time subsequent to when we speak, i.e., write, or even at the moment, even more subsequent, when we read, if this present "we" can even be uttered without creating confusion with the preceding "we," so it would probably be a good idea to say, or rather write, "when *you* read").

Now where izi tit that we're at, like my Mammary used to say?

We were on the subject of Laurie and Carlotta's persistent redheadedness and how the novel was justified in using "were" redheads (which, by the way, on reflection, doesn't strike me as so much more satisfactory, because I see no reason to suppose that Laurie and Carlotta [or Carlotta and Laurie]—who didn't cease being redheads between the moment of the Christmas shopping list scene and the next of writing the novel, or the next [or those] of reading it—are going to cease being redheads in the future, regardless whether this future concerns the moment of uttering and/or writing in question here, and consequently what perhaps ought to be said, written or thought is: "will be and will have been redheads").

To sum up, Laurie and Carlotta had been/were/are/will be/will have been redheads, and we can't overemphasize the risks such a feature entails for a narrator: a novelist with redheaded female characters is living dangerously, that's for sure.

Ophelia wasn't red-furred, but gray, soft gray. With blue eyes, soft blue.

She was momentarily worried because Laurie and Carlotta had got caught up in a discussion about complex numbers, and she was afraid that they'd forget about the shopping order, meaning that if the order wasn't handed over in time, the supply of cat food wouldn't be replenished and her dish would go empty, the thought of which threw her into an incredible panic. She meowed unobtrusively.

The panic sparked in Ophelia by her empty dish, even on a full belly (she who by nature was generally levelheaded and even-tempered), can be justified by her past history; the time has now come to set it down in black and white before your eyes, so I dare not delay giving you the facts a moment longer:

Ophelia was not the only, but no less beloved daughter of a Poldevian princess. During a picnic on the shores of Lake Melankton she was abducted from her tearful family by Poldadamian pirates who procured kittens for the slave markets of six continents; put on the auction block by her captors in a shady agency on Quai de la Moananmisery, she spent the first six months of her existence locked in a cage, from which Laurie and Carlotta delivered her by jumping into the bidding and beating out a very suspicious-looking Poldevian in whom we recognize an envoy of Prince Augre, the Demon Prince. From this experience Ophelia had retained:

—a feeling of eternal gratitude toward the two redheads;

—a panicky fear of not being fed.

Carlotta was explaining to her mother Laurie her recent discovery of complex numbers (to whom should such a discovery be confided if not one's mother?): "Isn't producing the root for -1 just wonderful?" she was saying. "Why shouldn't -1 have a root like 1 or 2 or any other number? Now I ask you." Laurie had a radical, or if you prefer, deep-rooted disinterest in complex numbers, and answered Carlotta the way Socrates does in Plato's dialogues, with "indeed"'s and "what's certain is that"'s and other onomatopoeias; she jotted down oregano after "termite salad" (for "taramasalata") on her shopping list. "And the complex plane," Carlotta said, "now I like the complex plane; each complex number has a real part and an imaginary part; when you get down to it, the imaginary part is the unconscious of complex numbers; it may even be that

61

the unconscious is structured like the complex plane; you lent me your gray pullover to go to the swimming pool." "Three baskets of cherry tomatoes," Laurie added onto the list. She ripped the sheets out of the notebook and handed them to Jim Wedderburn. "Excuse me? I lent you my gray pullover to go to the swimming pool? I've just about had it with you taking my things without asking!" Carlotta smiled. The bell rang announcing that the mail had arrived; it contained Hortense's letter.

"What a bimbo! What a total bimbo!" said Laurie and Carlotta after reading Hortense's letter. "What the hell is she doing mixed up in this business?"

Reaching number 8 of the excerpts singled out by Hortense from *Hortense in Exile,* the tale of her adventures, Laurie paused in thought; she moved on to excerpt number 9; at this point, all doubt had vanished: "Go get me letter *H* from the *Encyclopaedia Britannica,*" she told Carlotta. "Just as I thought," she said a little later, "she's gone and landed herself in *Hamlet!* What a bimbo! What a total bimbo!"

"What do you plan on doing?" Jim Wedderburn asked.

"Let her figure it out for herself," said Laurie and Carlotta at first. "She shouldn't have gone off to Poldevia anyway! How can somebody just go off to Poldevia? We're positive that redheads are persecuted in Poldevia: she should hop on the first plane out and come home and dump this prince of hers who's got this idea he's Hamlet and wants to avenge his father who got poisoned by the Reigning Prince and who (the Reigning Prince) then married his Mammumy; what business is that of hers?" said Carlotta and Laurie.

"Read all the way to the end," Jim Wedderburn advised.

Jim Wedderburn was Laurie's partner; together they had founded a very prosperous import-export firm trading in plastic bookstore bags; recently they had diversified, adding to their first range of selections plastic bags with authors' names and excerpts from their works, along with other innovations: for instance, that very morning, with Christmas around the corner, they were preparing for six Christmas Eve parties, the number of celebrations having been multiplied owing to the profusion of visits.

There was going to be: a holiday party for babies, thrown to celebrate the first meeting between Gaspard (three and two-thirds months old) and Laurie (a month younger—not of course the Laurie in the kitchen, drawing up the shopping list, but the one Carlotta has co-godmothered, in short S. and J-Y.'s daughter); as for Gaspard, he's the brother of Fanny (nine years old, whose cat, Miron, following two years of aborted efforts and ambushes has finally managed to gobble down the canaries, and who has just participated [Fanny, not her cat] on the pre-selection panel of judges for the Grand Prize in Adult Literature of Cachenaseau, on whose panel of finalists sits Jim Wedderburn who, completely unfamiliar with adult literature since he reads only books for children, in order to guide his own choice and votes, put together a pre-selection panel chaired by Ophelia: counting the ex-officio members, Laurie and Carlotta, the pre-selection panel totals four members; in the event of a draw [2 + 2 = 4, may I remind you], there's a tie-breaking half-vote that acts as a wild card, selected at random); Fanny came to collect in cheese the salary for her eminent contribution to the pre-selection panel's decisions;

—a party for Marion before she leaves for Saint-Gervais;

—a handsome-young-man's party;

—and all this before Carlotta herself leaves for her own New Year's Eve Party for Horses at Marina's, in Bruyères-les-Amoriques; Laurie had to finish up the costume Carlotta was going to wear for the event and blast every Bruyerois heart with her redheaded lightning (she had already stitched seven yards of hem on her sewing machine, reduced seven yards of pleats to six and a half feet [with six and a half still to be made and reduced to twenty-five inches, plus six and a half of tulle for the undergarment]; her costume at one point stretched around the entire kitchen; a black taffeta skirt with green polka dots [Note from Carlotta: I don't know if this is on purpose, but in reality it's a green taffeta skirt with black polka dots. Since the Author always tells the truth, and only the truth, I have to wonder.] above which was a Marilyn Monroesque long-line strapless black bra baring her shoulders ["It stopped," Laurie said, "right above Carlotta's little boobies," her daughter being seventeen years old]). Seeing that the year comes to an end in wintertime, Carlotta would also be provided with a wrap made of plastic velvet-sponge.

Jim Wedderburn was to accompany them to the Marché des Bébés Oranges for those items on the list they couldn't order through their Minitel shopping service; afterward, he would go with Laurie and Ophelia to the opening of the mail envelopes exhibition (a new form of pictorial art) by Laure Durien at Griffures Bookstore on Rue Vieille-des-Archives, before Laurie went off to her French boxing lesson (she was already a "green glove," but hoped to move up any day now to a "red").

"Go ahead and read," said Jim Wedderburn.

"I see," said Laurie in English, after finishing. "Whether Gormanskoï thinks he's Hamlet, or other people do, makes little difference; the consequence is that he along with others ('others' being Poldevia in general) take his fiancée Hortense for Hamlet's fiancée in the Shahkayspear play, and that's bad news, that's real bad news."

"As you say," Jim Wedderburn said.

"Whazgon'on?" Carlotta asked, who had only a passing admiration for Shahkayspear, preferring Molière, Morley's Theorem and Disassociribbonnonnucleahick acids along with other tiny voracious N-zymes.

"Well, in the play, Hamlet's fiancée goes mad and ends up drowned, that's what; being the complete airhead she is we wouldn't want Hortense to go and catch pneumonia."

"Someone," said Jim Wedderburn, "has instructed me to talk you into doing something to help Hortense; otherwise the novel's kaput."

"Couldn't this 'someone' come and ask in person?" Laurie said.

"You know full well," Jim Wedderburn said, "that a certain 'someone' can't intervene in the novel; the publisher has forbidden him. Anyway 'someone' is having domestic troubles."

"What kind of 'domestic troubles' can bachelors have?" Carlotta said.

"Oh well, you know, plumbing problems. His sink's leaking; he can't stick more than one pot at a time underneath given how the pipework's put together, and since it's a small leak, he doesn't get to stay out for more than six hours at a time whenever he wants to leave."

"Couldn't he turn off the water whenever he's not home, for instance?" said Carlotta. "Or call a plumber, for another instance?"

"True," said Jim Wedderburn, "but it probably hasn't occurred to him. Well, anyway," he continued, "you're leaving for Poldevia to get Hortense out of her mess, right?"

Part Three

*Once the Melodrama Gets Going
There's a Flood of Weapons*

Chapter 13

"You lose a few marbles, or what? You think we'd go off and bury ourselves for six months in Poldevia to get that airhead Hortense out of where she's gone and got herself in a jam all over again? First of all, who's got the time? Next, we don't like Poldevia. Speaking for myself, I'd go for a weekend at the max, all expenses paid. But don't count on Carlotta. This year she's starting work on her Ph.D. in Boogie-boarding on the San Diego campus," said Laurie.

"But I've been told by 'somebody' that if necessary . . .," Jim Wedderburn said, bending to whisper in the two redheads' ears.

The eyes of the three persons seated around the kitchen table rose in unison and turned toward the top of the cabinet above the refrigerator.

Ophelia was surprised. Adding the cat food to the grocery list had set her mind at rest, and she was only vaguely following the conversation. She couldn't quite decide what sort of a look to adopt. Among her extensive repertoire of expressions she had two favorites: innocence and obfuscation. She would put on her innocent look whenever she had:

1) crushed the house plants, or

2) swiped the salmon from the table, or

3) emptied the cupboard to find a packet that might contain valerian, or

4) turned Laurie's desk into a disaster area (it was impossible to reduce Carlotta's to rubble since it was a permanent shambles), or

5) stashed one of Laurie's pens in her war chest, and she saw

beforehand that one of the incidents covered by 1) 2) 3) 4) 5) was about to be discovered, thereby denying in advance any responsibility;

and she put on her look of obfuscation whenever she had

1) attacked the house plants, or

2) swiped the salmon from the table, or

3) emptied the cupboard to find the packet of valerian, or

4) turned Laurie's desk into a heap of ruins (it was impossible to reduce Carlotta's to rubble, since it was a permanent shambles), or

5) stashed one of Laurie's pens in her war chest, and she sensed that one of the incidents included in 1) 2) 3) 4) 5) had already been discovered and she was about to be accused.

Since the current situation fit into neither of these two categories, she didn't know quite what to make of these stares converging upon her, and she felt uneasy.

"Read this," Carlotta said, holding out Hortense's letter.

Let's leave these characters in their perplexity, a state both decisive and indecisive (we can't overemphasize how much the story's harmonious progress hinges on the outcome; we hope that Laurie and Carlotta will consider their responsibilities) midway through Chapter 13 (the chapter's title, "Chapter 13," matches its contents rather well; better, in any case, than "Chapter 12," or "Epilogue")—and let's go back to Poldevia where we left Hortense, finishing her letter, in the middle of the last page of Chapter 11.

A short time, almost one full night, has passed.

(From Hortense's diary: a few fragments from the diary kept by Hortense in Poldevia have been located; the Author seems to have been unaware of this diary's existence. *Publisher's note.*)

I had a weird dream during the night: I was in bed, chatting with Alexandre Vladimirovitch, when Prince Augre came into the room; but he wasn't interested in me. In his company were six sturdy moving men who began to load the furniture onto their shoulders and backs. When they reached the bed I got up without paying him any mind and put on my dressing gown. Just then my own prince came over and said, "Hortense, go to bed." They fought the whole time, with Gormanskoï repeating: "Hortense, go to bed!" This description captures my situation fairly well, it seems to me.

Morning has come again, with Christmas now around the corner. Hortense comes back with croissants and a brioche for Alexandre Vladimirovitch (who eats only the tender innards, with a splash of milk); she has put on her Welsh oilskin because of the downpour. In her hand she is holding her coin, a gold piece worth one Poldevian guinea. She passes her fingers over the numbers running around the rim of the hexagon—the 6, the 5, the 4, the 3, the 2, and the 1, slightly scratched so that it looks like an "i"; she goes through the heavy wire mesh door of Sainte-Gudule Cathedral Park; the sun is shining, the birds are singing; yes, read closely, and let me repeat: the sun is shining, the birds are singing. She rubs the Poldevian guinea in her hand, runs her fingers across the numbers decorating the hexagonal rim: the 1, the 2, the 3, the 5, the 6, and the 4, split in two, with the vertical bar removed, so that the only part left is the "<" sign. She walks up to the entrance to the Gormanskoï Palace, at the corner of the angle formed by the hexarchy's six palaces; it faces Sainte-Gudule; Alexandre Vladimirovitch holds out her key, small and flat, encrusted with a blue sapphire; just as she is about to open the door, three men in blue, wearing ski masks, spring out, grab Hortense, and drag her off. Alexandre Vladimirovitch escapes the abductors.

(Meanwhile, in a small inn in a small town in the Poldevian province.) Breakfast—a traditional complete Poldevian breakfast—has just ended for the two stout, hearty, middle-aged men sitting in the entrance-hall armchairs: a nice plateful of boutifara with gooseberry jam, six eggs with bacon, a stack of six pancakes covered with boysenberry syrup, etc. They were sitting calmly and kindly disposed in the entrance hall of the Red Inn (for such was the name of this small hotel) and each was waiting: one, for his mother; the other, his wife. The two women have gone up to their rooms in order to change for the day's outing, a "peek-neek" on Lake Melankton on whose shore sits the hotel. One of the two gentlemen, the one waiting for his spouse, takes out of his pocket a package of Callard and Bowser's licorice, the best in the world, and prepares to enjoy his first stick of the day. As the reader has guessed, the two men are none other than the famous Inspector Blognard, the most celebrated of our policemen, and his assistant, Inspector Arapède. They are vacationing in Poldevia.

They continue waiting; and while waiting, they philosophize, which is the normal thing to do in such circumstances.

More often than not, Arapède takes a skeptical stance; he's a great admirer of Sextus Empiricus and Chillingworth; he has brought along on vacation with him a new work, *Ignorance* by Peter Unger, packed with a good many anticipated delights. And, as a matter of fact, he had just gotten to the point in his reading where Mr. Unger, having employed new, modern linguistic arguments in order to establish to Arapède's satisfaction as well as to his own that we are unable to know anything with any degree of certainty about the outside world, states: "If I can *never come to know anything* about the outside world— not even whether or not there is one—how can I have *one single reason* to believe something about the world; about a world? The truth becomes evident to me, at the end of this investigation, that *any such thing is impossible,* if I *know* nothing certain. And since I've been inevitably forced to conclude that indeed I *can* know nothing about an outside world, in consequence it does seem I can have *no reasonable belief,* at least on this subject."

Blognard, as always, meets him with a good-natured retort. Inspector Arapède is a fine, conscientious detective who can easily be granted his few philosophic idiosyncracies.

"Do you believe," Arapède said, "in Lewis's reality of the plurality of possible worlds?"

"Are you talking about the plurality of possible worlds belonging to Lewis?"

"No, no, I'm talking about the theory of David Lewis who believes not only in the reality of our world, but in those realities of a plurality (potentially, or even actually infinite) of possible worlds; as Mr. Lewis himself points out, he is a confirmed modal realist."

"Do you mean that he believes in worlds in which there might be winged horses, talking asses, and in which Ph****** S******, for example, would be even more intelligent and more talented than Victor Mature, for instance?"

"Yes."

"Could be, could be," Blognard said, chewing on a new piece of licorice. "I believe that it's possible for other possible worlds to exist, but I wouldn't stake my life on it."

Then Arapède launched into a scathing refutation of Lewis's theories, throwing out notions like *haesseitas,* the Principle of Indiscernibles, transworldly identities, etc.—remarks to which Blognard gave only his rather divided attention; but he started listening again when Arapède broached the question of Poldevia's reality: "Do you really believe in Poldevia's existence?"

"I can't see any way around it, since I'm Inspector Blognard and I'm vacationing in this country."

Arapède smiled at this feeble argument.

"Let's be serious: how can you be so certain? Because you are not in a possible or hypothetical Poldevia, but in a novel where it is postulated, as a necessary truth, i.e., true in every possible world, that Poldevia exists, and that we are at present visiting it? But can a novel, which you'll grant me is something necessarily contingent (go and ask publishers, go and ask bookstore

73

owners)—can a novel contain the slightest necessary truth? I suppose you're familiar with the Evil Demon argument: isn't your conviction that the world exists an illusion inspired by the demon who is amusing himself by making you believe just that?"

"Yes, but," Blognard interjected, "the Evil Demon can't make me falsely believe in my own existence since, in order for me to believe something, I do really need to exist in order to believe it."

"OK," Arapède said, "you think, therefore you are, OK. That's not what I'm talking about; in our present situation, don't you think we'd be perfectly capable of defending the hypothesis that such an Evil Demon exists, and that this Evil Demon is none other than the Author himself? You know, or believe you do, based on an inner conviction, that you exist, you've read *Our Beautiful Heroine* and *Hortense Is Abducted,* two novels which talk about you. But have you the slightest self-knowledge outside of what's written there?"

"Yes, but," Blognard said, "can your Evil Demon make me believe that he made me believe in the reality of the world described in the novel I'm in?"

Arapède seemed not to have listened to this objection, which as a matter of fact we ourselves don't understand, but instead went on: "I think—as I've often told you—that reasonable beliefs don't exist; but in any case, for you as well as for myself, there do exist *unreasonable beliefs.* Is it *reasonable* to believe that Poldevian princes exist who are mutually indiscernible in every feature except for a design, some birthmark on their left buttock, a stylized depiction of a snail (three of which are dextrogyrous, or twisting to the right; and three, levogyrous, or twisting to the left—a fact the Author neglects to clarify)? Furthermore, is it reasonable that the same situation is duplicated for each generation, regardless of the respective mothers and fathers? Isn't it more plausible, just simply plausible, to think that all of Poldevia came into existence just one moment ago, with the first words of this book, and will disappear (and ourselves along with it, and its readers) once the book is over? I'll possibly grant you Poldevia's existence in the two novels I've mentioned earlier, provided that they never were and are not just merely a trick of the Author, falsely convincing you that you've read them. But perhaps even Poldevia's disappearance, and our own along with it, and your wife's and my poor mother's are all hanging on one simple gesture—turning the present page of *Hortense in Exile.*"

Blognard immediately turned the page, and they didn't disappear.

"That just proves," Arapede said, "a certain singlemindedness on the Author's part, nothing more, nothing more."

"But all of this," Blognard said, "doesn't establish the fact that I'm a bicycle."

"Of course," Arapede said. "So what?"

Blognard's wife and Arapede's mother were making their way down the stairs.

Chapter 14

On Lake Melankton

"In any case," Blognard said later, as he listened to their boatman, a fellow by the name of Chaliapinskoï, singing "*e e oukhniem, e e oukh-niem ie tcho ra- a -zik ie-e tcho raz*" in a beautiful, deep bass voice while pushing their boat along the waters of Lake Melankton with his pole, "the Poldevians look like they firmly believe in Poldevia's existence."

"Where are we right at the moment, my good man?" Arapède said.

"In Poldadamia, my dear sir, on Lake Melankton."

Blognard made no reply. He was deep in thought. As soon as they got into the boat, he had received a telegram written in secret code which left him pensive (it had been sent by Alexandre Vladimirovitch from the main post office on Place Queneleieff).

"This Lewis of yours," he said, "the one who believes in all those worlds, does he think that several separate worlds can coexist?"

"No," Arapède answered, "he refutes what's called 'overlap'; but the theory has many defenders: it's what's called the *hypothesis of compossible worlds*. Needless to say I myself don't subscribe to it."

The boat glided across the water, calm and therefore deep blue; some distance away stood an island surmounted by a dark fortress. The boatman scowled, pointing at the island with his pole:

"Bad, that place, bad; *kakashkaia!*"

Let's be frank. When Laurel and Hardy, while supposedly at

76

some business convention, are spotted on a movie screen by the wives they've left behind, joyfully roving the streets of Honolulu in the company of charming, fetching, scantily clad "ukulele babies," it is totally pointless for them to try and cover up their heinous crime once they get back to their respective homes. Although in vain Laurel stubbornly insists on denying the fact, Hardy by contrast confesses right away and as a reward is immediately forgiven: "Honesty," he tells Laurel, "honesty is the best policy!"

Novelists are faced with a similar dilemma: having gone off for a good time instead of soberly making deals (what's termed in novel theory "composing a real literary work"), he must choose one of two paths: Laurel's or Hardy's. We choose honesty, in the cautiously held hope of some reward.

This is why we also are not going out of our way to conceal the glaring truth: yes, Poldevia is a multiple world; in the hexarchy there are not only six principalities, six princes, but six worlds, of the coexisting, "compossible" sort Inspector Arapède was just talking about a few lines back. These worlds are in appearance very similar, but are radically different in essence, in their moral "makeup," along with a few significant details (numismatic, pictorial, and climatic). If you are in World #1, the world of truth and beauty and goodness, the world of Hortense's fiancé, Prince Airt'n, whose color is red, whose gold coins worth one Poldevian guinea have their number 1 slightly scratched to make it look like an "i," a mere trifle can propel you into the evil, diabolical alternate world inhabited by Prince Augre, who lusts after Hortense, and into whose clutches she fell on crossing through a metal gate. The color of this world is blue, the beneficial rain gives way to sniggering sunshine, the gold coins have their number 4 so cut as to reveal a "$<$," the mathematical symbol of lesser value! Of course there are four other worlds, about which we'll say nothing for the moment to avoid getting ahead of ourselves; for the novel tells what it must, when it must, and never sooner or later.

And now the novel, spreading its cards of frankness and candor upon the table, is telling us that Hortense was being held prisoner on an island in Lake Melankton, amid the rough, treacherous waters of that section of the lake almost exclusively situated in Prince Augre's world. Arapède and Blognard had just rowed unawares very close by their fellow citizen, whose kidnapping they nevertheless knew about. For why hide it? Alexandre Vladimirovitch's telegram had removed all doubt; in a flash, based on the telegraphic report of the circumstantial evidence, Blognard had deduced the single solution that satisfied all the data: the compossibility of worlds. And the question he had put to the boatman Chaliapinskoï, a typical representative, as it were, of the Poldevian people in all their basic simplicity, was not intended to further an easy dialectic victory for Inspector Arapède (he knew everything about Chaliapinskoï, even before hiring his boat for the "peekneek"), but rather to verify another hypothesis he had formulated, namely, that the majority of Poldevians who aren't princes and who are honest *don't believe* in the existence of six co-worlds inhabited by themselves; and *not one person knows* that there are, in fact, six of them. You'll agree that Blognard deduced this swiftly!

As we've said, the six worlds are in close proximity to each other: in space-time they all occupy the exact same points; in addition they are somewhat intimately bound by history since they are no more different today than they were six centuries ago when Prince Arnaut Danielskoï founded the Hexarchy. We can postulate therefore that this "chronoclastic infidibulum" possesses a certain solidity, but we'll leave the task of formulating the equations to cosmogonists.

Hence, we can rightly dismiss the blatantly inadequate, radical hypothesis postulating the coexistence in the same place and time not just of six worlds (as we've asserted about Poldevia), but of as many worlds as there are individuals; worlds mutually unknowable with ubiquitous, impassable borders. This is the multisolipsistic thesis that one day Laurie formulated as follows: "You can never be two people at once in the same movie" (moreover, she added right afterward: "I do know somebody who thinks he's Morris in the cat food commercial!"). But by contrast we should also stress that this means each of these worlds doesn't exist in a state of total autonomy. What happens in one inevitably has repercussions in the others. Nor are there twice as many (I mean six as many) objects, entities, or creatures which make up each world. They're all the same; their combinations change with hardly anything material being lost or created. It's not another Hortense who is once again in the clutches of the man she once knew under the accursed name of K'manoroïgs (now Augre), but the very same woman we've known, with her overly sexy shapes, her unwitting bimbotude, her skimpy, exciting panties, her passion for Gormanskoï and for philosophy! She is now in the blue world of treason, having left the red world, the world of happiness!

Chapter 15

The Prisoneress of Zenda

Clinging to Cyrandzoï's mane and protected from the water by his heat-retentive frog-catsuit, under the cover of darkness Alexandre Vladimirovitch was swept past every obstacle, every trap (the demon's "complete regalia," as Father Risolnus would have put it) toward the fortress of Zenda where Hortense was being held. One after the other the pony crossed the six rings of water cutting the fortress off from the continent. Zenda wasn't simply an island in Lake Melankton; on the island itself there was a pond, and in this pond a pool, and in this pool yet another pool, and in this other pool, a third, and only there, at last, separated off by a deep treacherous moat, loomed the tall stone tower of Zenda! And as for the difficulty in getting from one ring to the next, well, you haven't heard the half of it! In short, you won't be hearing much of anything about it, since I'd rather stay with Alexandre Vladimirovitch who, completely relying on Cyrandzoï, is making an effort not to dwell on these expanses of watery wetness and to turn his mind instead to working out some rescue plans.

On one side of the drawbridge over the moat (or "ditch" surrounding the castle that belongs to the Prince who fears neither God nor man) rose a stone staircase with thirty-seven steps (of which two were twice as high as the others) leading to two small rooms carved directly out of the rock. The steps led to the nearest room, windowless and candlelit twenty-four hours a day. The other room had one small window looking out onto the ditch. In the first room three of the Prince's six most reliable men took turns maintaining an around-the-clock guard. The

Prince had ordered that if this first room were attacked, they should defend the door as long as possible; but if they saw that the door was about to be forced open, somebody ought to dash into the second room, seize Hortense, and toss her into the pipe.

What pipe? The one blocking up the room's window, a large pipe made out of Sèvres porcelain on which a false window, panes and all, had been painted in trompe l'oeil, plunging straight down into the moat, running beneath the ditch floor, then re-emerging in a third room where the Prince had set up headquarters. After Hortense was tossed into the pipe, but before the attackers had set foot in the now empty room, one of the criminal's confederates was to pull a lever which would snap off the pipe and send it crashing into the watery moat, thus unblocking the window. The apparently empty room would dupe Gormanskoï's men (which is who they'd obviously be), forcing them to report back to their leader that the woman they had hoped to rescue had inexplicably vanished. This was the setup Alexandre Vladimirovitch inspected that night. He sneaked inside, saw what there was to see, rode back the way he came on Cyrandzoï, and gave a complete rundown to Prince Acrab'm, placed by his ally in charge of Hortense's commando of liberators.

The room holding Hortense prisoner was small but comfortable; it was a more cramped version of her bathroom in the palace, with one added feature: a cot in the corner. After shouting in vain, ranting and raving, attempting and failing to understand what was going on, Hortense tried to console herself by doing what she always did in moments of duress: she decided to take a bath. She ran water into the tub, slipped her skirt down to her feet, her sweater up over her head, and then nimbly took off a pair of skimpy blue silk panties (Hortense breaks in: "The Reader won't get any further details: enough's been said about what's covering my bottom; from here on I'm censoring."). She was completely stripped to the skin. Testing the temperature with her foot and judging it acceptable, she placed her second foot into the tub and eased herself down into the comforting water with a sigh of relief. Her hand, still clutching the soap but moving away from her thighs, now a slightly paler shade of caramel (since the last of her baths we attended, whose description we'll pick up right at the spot on Hortense's body where we left off; all Hortense's baths follow the same unchanging ritual), gravitated toward the dual hemispheres resting on her chest. Hortense's breasts, whose surface equation was precisely calculated by the Prince's mathematicians according to measurements taken by the Prince in person from his live model (and we can divulge that this surface isn't algebraic but transcendental) are on the small side, although very smooth, firm, and round all at once. She has extremely sensitive nipples. In the same way that the famous Magdeburg Hemispheres placed on top of each other in empty space can't be pulled apart by forty horses, so Hortense's breasts stand with stubborn pride upon her chest. Hortense took them in her hands, weighed them, soaped them, played with their tips (although momentarily fooled by her palm, they quickly understood they weren't in the Prince's hands). "Ah," Hortense thought, closing her eyes, "if only I could open my eyes and discover this has all been some nightmare, that I'm back in my bathtub in the palace with Alexandre Vladimirovitch sitting on the rim." She opened her eyes, and there sat Alexandre Vladimirovitch.

"Shh!" Alexandre Vladimirovitch motioned with his paw against his whiskers.

He vanished at once, but Hortense sensed that her rescue was in the works, which reassured her a little.

But not for long. She had just finished up with her breasts and was moving her soapy hands down over her belly when the door opened and Prince Augre walked in. Hortense saw right away that he was Prince Augre and she realized she was done for. Alexandre Vladimirovitch would probably manage to get back to Gormanskoi, who would dash off to her rescue; and he would rescue her, she was sure about that; but not in time. She was about to be inflicted with the **Absolute Shame** from which she had escaped in the nick of time during her preceding adventure (relayed with unsurpassable suspense in the novel *Hortense Is Abducted*); she made up her mind to exact a high price for her flesh, at least that part of her flesh in question. And, who knows, maybe buy some time as well? Jab him with her knee, perhaps? Her hand clutched the bar of soap.

Prince Augre glared at Hortense long and hard with all his ignoble desire; like some lubricious snail his eyes spiraled through the soapy water to profane our heroine's innocent charms. In spite of herself, her hands dropped to cover that smallish, grassy-looking, triangular area, the tiniest territory in the world, which has been the subject of poets' songs and so many knights' battles. As a result her breasts were left undefended; they tried disappearing into Hortense's chest; but in vain, their volume couldn't be compressed, nor their form deformed; the criminal's stare slithered across them.

Slowly, ironically, taking his time, sure of his triumph, the Prince untied his blue Japanese-print pattern kimono. It slipped down off his shoulders, his hips; fell to the floor, to his feet. He stood naked. He had Gormanskoi's good looks, but was as handsome as the Devil himself; Hortense felt nothing but disgust, fury, and loathing. She looked away from the sorry spectacle of that perpendicularity preparing to perpetrate violence upon her. Not a single word had passed their lips.

Then the Prince entered the tub and an awful struggle began, a series of defeats, strategic retreats replete with gaasps, ssplashes, grrowls, mooans, sllippingandslliding; Hortense, like Monsieur Seguin's goat in another set of circumstances and with something else at stake, fought back, back, one hour, nearly two; but little by little her strength petered out; the Prince was upon her, pinning her body motionless; she was done for.

But no!

Just at the point when he might have been able to experience the thrill of victory, he lost the desire; conquering her wasn't enough, he wanted her to *ask* him to be conquered: "The day will come," he told her insolently, "the day will come when you beg me to give you what today I could take if I chose; but I don't deign to. See you soon."

In such language does pride express and reveal its awful monomania. Who will ever be able to recount the ravages of what in the past was called hubris? In a similar situation (minus the preliminaries and their moral implications; I just want to consider Hortense's ultimate situation, defenseless, delivered into her enemy's hands by chance, let's say) who would have turned away? You?

Augre walked out on Hortense, who was left exhausted, humiliated, gasping for breath, but unsullied.

Chapter 16

The Fake Hortense

Hortense's defeat and humiliation were horrible to be sure, but neither was total nor final; at least she had bought some time. Alerted by Alexandre Vladimirovitch, the Prince (if he was indeed the person who had masterminded the cat's appearance on the bathtub rim) would be doing everything in his power to snatch her from the claws of her abductor. She didn't believe— she didn't want to!—that just because he took himself for some revenge-obsessed Hamlet he was going to neglect her like some new Ophelia, thus dooming her honor—such a sad thought!— to "muddy death" (also part of the Demon Prince's plan once he accomplished what he had set out to do). And so, sleepless upon her hard narrow prison cot, our heroine Hortense see-sawed from hope to despair, and from despair back to hope.

What's coming next will probably strike some readers as exorbitantly "medieval," if not outright "Gothic"; but the novel's synopsis makes it mandatory and there's nothing we can do about it. If you insist, be my guest and construct a symbolic or allegorical interpretation of the scene about to be described; or you're most welcome to skip ahead to the next scene instead: I for one will not stray one inch from my path: I will tell what happened because happen it did.

By leaving his victim unconsummated. Prince Augre was, as we've already said, probably yielding to some impulse of pride, a flair for the outrageous, marked by a touch of magnanimity, a reaction which moreover leaves some hope in the Reader's heart for a happy resolution. We should point out in this connection that there's no possible way for us to know how things will turn out; we aren't striking one of those disingenuous poses that the previous decision to be absolutely frank à la Oliver Hardy would force us to turn over like a new leaf (*attention reviewers:* to avoid confusion we should explain that "turning over a new leaf" is an idiomatic expression signifying a change in behavior and/or attitude, symbolized by a fresh sheet or "leaf" of paper); not by any means; we're keeping quiet because everything is still up in the air. The narrative future, like the future plain and simple, is always a future perfect; it's only after the last page with "The End" has been turned and the book closed that we will be able to say: **It was written!** But for the moment it's not.

So then, Prince Augre had acted out of pride; but also out of vanity, which sure as hell isn't the same thing. In reality, he couldn't imagine that Hortense, being female, therefore full of lust like all females, was really going to resist his charms; as a matter of fact, during their recent encounter, it was surely his surprise more than anything else which led him at the very last second to deny the immense desire she was experiencing **in reality** (this is the monster thinking—*novel's note*) deep in her innermost recesses where every woman alive can't keep her mind off of HIM. Indeed there was no other possible alternative. Wasn't he an exact lookalike of Gormanskoï, but just more inwardly accomplished, more authentically Poldevian (and noncosmopolitan), more manly? No: the struggle put up by Hortense was a mere ploy, a typical feminine means of whetting his appetite; oh well, he'd make her wait, and in the end she'd come to him naked on her knees, imploring him to fulfill her.

Once he had thought this all through, the Prince's sexual juices started flowing again furiously, sapping his strength. So he decided to go down into what he called his "picture chamber," a cave carved into the granitic foundation ("granitic" refers to granite mixed with blue chalk—*Encyclopaedia Poldevica*) of Zenda. Here he collected photos, audiocassettes, and videos of all his conquests, which he liked to feast on for relaxation. He filled the walls with life-size pictures of Hortense as nature had made her, taken in her prison cell where she was being filmed round-the-clock by invisible cameras (which Alexandre Vladimirovitch, although spotting and ducking them, was unable to hinder from doing their sinister duty for fear of attracting the criminal's attention. He made do with disabling a couple of the more indiscreetly positioned lenses by pissing on them).

So down into his picture chamber went the Prince to take the edge off; but wherever he looked the flatness of Hortense's depictions (her "pictions" we might say), including the ones endowed with motion, left him unsatisfied. Grabbing hold of a hunk of mostly flesh-colored modeling clay he set about fashioning a Hortense-size doll as identical as possible to its model. In memory and his mind's eye he could see her from enough different angles and perspectives to recall every least detail. He worked through the night and, at dawn, the replica was ready. The resemblance was breathtaking; the buttocks in particular, the buttocks! . . . But let's not get carried away, this is just a fiction, a phantasm, a pale reflection. The Prince was so astounded by the resemblance that lust swept through him again with a raw, more awful violence; without a second's further thought he pounced and started knowing her in the biblical sense; and she actually responded to his caresses! to his hugs!! wrapped her legs of now firm modeling clay around him!!! they've become fleshlike!!!! with her hand she guided him toward!!!!! . . . between!!!!!! and even between . . ., etc. A miracle —a Satanic miracle—had taken place. The FAKE HORTENSE was born.

As quickly as we can, let's break our absorption and tear our degrading imaginations away from this unwholesome spectacle in order to rejoin Alexandre Vladimirovitch, presently removing his frog-catsuit with extreme care, then shaking it completely dry without getting a single drop of water on himself. While Cyrandzoï was galloping along the lakeshore, fluttering his russet mane and splattering the poppies (poppies in wintertime? why yes: they're a species of the *Poppaveraceae* native to Poldevia which blossom every December. In the words of the poet: "A poppy 'n Decemb'r is more exquisite by far"), Al. Vl. reports to Gormanskoï and Inspector Blognard (less than an hour has passed since Inspector Blognard was assigned this Case with in-ter-*na*-tion-al implications. A copy of the exact wording of the recent extradition treaties between our country and the Hexarchy was telexed to him immediately).

Contrary to Hortense's foreboding, the Prince wasn't so hopelessly spellbound by the problems of Poldevian succession that he stopped caring about his fiancée's welfare. He needed to act quickly, all the more so since he himself most probably was going to be a long way from the theater of operations soon. Of course the most pressing task was to fill in Laurie and Carlotta on the latest developments (we've omitted Ophelia for a simple reason which we'll get to later). And to whom other than to Alexandre Vladimirovitch could such a mission be entrusted? As a matter of fact, no one. "Go," said the Prince.

He went.

(From Hortense's diary [cf. Chapter 13]: Prince Augre came; he was indeed my abductor; I might have guessed; he barged in, with his eyes popping from his head, right in the middle of my bath, and naturally he tried to rape me; in my adventures there are—let me just say this in passing—a certain number of individuals who are all fixated on one thing: sleeping with me, with or without my consent [and I am rather afraid that among this number I have to include both the Author and the Reader; fortunately there are perhaps a few female readers who've got other things on their minds]. So he tried and failed miserably. Regardless of how much he looks like Gormanskoï, I don't like him; and I absolutely hate it when I'm not asked permission. He walked straight into the water stark naked. I had a good laugh because he looked so totally ridiculous and it would have been so awkward! He seemed very miffed, and I thought he'd give up the idea on his own; but since he kept at it I was forced to be pretty mean and he left yelling. I'll be glad when Alexandre Vladimirovitch gets back with my Prince. It isn't even comfortable here.)

Chapter 17

Scribbled in the Theater

(For this chapter—in other respects rather second-rate—the novelist has left only an outline which we will reproduce to the best of our abilities: the wealth of material was such that its sheer size would have gone beyond the limits of what anyone could stand to read.)

The scene takes place in the theater of Eërlosni Castle, on Place Queneleieff, occupied by the usurping Reigning Prince, Alcius, and his accomplice, Gertrude, mother of Gormanskoï, alas!

The action begins—if we are correctly deciphering the rather sloppy pencil-written manuscript—with Gorm-Ham in a conversation with Gertrude; she receives him in her dressing room (?) (she is playing in something? *Hamlet?*); a portrait of Gertrude, her large stone face; and in the dressing room, paintings by Picasso (?); incomprehensible mutterings from Gertrude; something about "pigeons on the grass, alas! pigeons on the grass, alas!" (as rendered by a translator whose name is illegible, but in all probability a member of the Translation Commission of the NCPPL, National Center for Poldevian and Poldadamian Letters); a fragment of dialogue:

GERTR: "Gormie, thou hast thy father much offended."

GORM: "Mother, you have my father much offended."

(The above probably rendered by the same translator mentioned above.)

Then Gorm hears a sound: a rat? Alexandre Vladimirovitch isn't around to hunt it down; G. draws his sword, thrusts it into the orange drapes; it's Poldevius, the prime minister; he moans and expires.

(The draft, still abridged but in uninterrupted form, picks up at this point; we should however observe that it's no doubt a rough draft incorporating encyclopedia-like passages.)

Hatmel, one of the most famous plays in Poldevia's theatrical repertoire, and *Hamlet,* a rather inferior rendition preserved in the even more inferior version by the Englishman William Shahykayspear, share an identical source in a passage from the twelfth-century *Historiae Poldeviae* by Polo Poldevicus. Adaptations for the stage had been circulating throughout Europe since the sixteenth century. The *Ur-Hatmel,* which Shahykayspear certainly used, has not been preserved, but in any case *Hatmel* owes nothing to the English author (the opposite is far more likely), a fact particularly evident in the hero's name, Hatmel, which is the Poldevian form of Amleth, the character's name in the story by Polo Poldevicus (the Poldevian form of Hamlet would naturally be Theal'm).

In order to get a better feel for what it's like to watch a performance in the grand theater of Eërlosni Castle it's important for you to keep in mind a few typical features of contemporary stagecraft in Poldevia. It's common knowledge that Poldevia was the first country to experience the full throes of the *theater crisis* which to this day has the rest of the civilized world still reeling. A commission assembled from representatives of all concerned professions (therefore excluding reviewers, who are concerned with anything and everything but the theater)— namely, authors, directors, politicians, actors, theatergoers, bakers, prompters, set designers, trash collectors—met over a three-year period at a round, hexagonal table, interrogated thousands of witnesses, attended hundreds of shows, then ended up by proposing a certain number of measures that have presently been adopted on an experimental basis in our country.

The issue had been raised, for example, that actors, unlike musicians, were obliged to remain in the same theater for the entire duration of the performance of any play in which they

91

had a part. While the other actors spoke and broke their concentration (trying to make them forget their lines) they were sometimes forced to spend small eternities waiting around for their turns like porcelain vases. So it was proposed that actors should make their stage appearances in succession and deliver *all their lines at one go,* take a bow, wait for the applause, then be on their way (for example, to perform *another* role in *another* theater). *Bérénice* by Pierre Corneille (?) was performed in such a way recently and met with a huge popular success (the members of the audience having one favorite performer and zero interest in anybody else are free to follow the actors' example).

Elsewhere in the report the point was made that actors should show more deference toward the audience; not everybody can hold the program either in front of their eyes, or in memory, and tell "who's who" without some reminder. Therefore it was deemed absolutely necessary that before delivering their lines, all actors ought to identify themselves by giving their names and the role they were supposed to be playing: "Ph****** S****** in the role of Cleopatra," for example. A perhaps more preferable variation would entrust the duty of making introductions to another actor, who might for example say to the audience: "Madame Pâquerette d'Azur in the role of Phèdre." Or: "And now you will hear—if he can remember his lines— Father Risolnus, who jumped at the chance to play Falstaff."

One of the most considerable benefits of this reform would be the reassurance the actors themselves receive about their own identities.

If the audience's comfort and a smoothly flowing performance are given genuine priority, it goes without saying how vital it is to provide exact, precise information about what's going on in order to avoid confusion. For example, when a stage set replicates the directions set down by the author at the beginning of each act, it was suggested this description should be delivered out loud by the actors as they themselves became acquainted with the location where they are supposed to be performing. The audience, simultaneously following the set along with its eyes while listening to the presentation, will then be free to focus on the actors instead of wandering off into the drapery. (A certain avant-garde author, always on the lookout for a chance to do mischief, recently deconstructed this excellent innovation in the most treacherous way. In his play, whose set depicts an unpeopled mountain landscape, the first actor on stage starts as follows: "The set depicts a seaside resort; in the foreground, on the sand, a row boat"; and then he points at a bike!)

So then, the truth, always the truth, the brutal truth. The result (and this now concerns the author) is that if something is said to the audience, whatever is said must *necessarily be true.* This is part of the pact established between author and viewer, between mouth and ear. It's under this express condition that trust will be reestablished between the theater and its public; furthermore, if you put yourself in the actor's shoes you should have no trouble seeing that since he is talking on stage alone (for the moment let's assume that the public remains silent) his lines in many respects resemble a soliloquy, i.e., a speech you deliver to yourself; now I ask you, is it conceivable, is it even possible (so read the report) to consciously and intentionally say something to yourself that you know to be false? Obviously not!

You mustn't believe that all these rules, basically no more than guidelines, will unduly hamper the freedom of directors: not only will they retain a vast area for maneuvering, but with a spark of imagination they'll be able to display more creativity than ever before. A performance of *The Misanthrope,* for instance, might begin as follows:

> Yes, since I find again so true a friend,
> Fortune's about to take a different turn.

Now, for your average theatergoer, *ça va;* since he's come to hear *The Misanthrope,* directed by M.A.V. (let's suppose), then what he'll hear will be *The Misanthrope* as directed by

M.A.V. But some exceptionally astute members of the audience will not fail to discover that, although the title of the performance is *The Misanthrope,* the text being acted is *Andromache,* and as the show wears on they'll admire the surplus of theatrical meaning which M.A.V. creates by virtue of this transposition. For he sets up extremely illuminating parallels between the friends Orestes and Pylades on the one hand, Alceste and Philinte on the other. Term for term the projected correspondences (underscored by a handful of basically minor script changes, fine-tuned daily) between Molière's and Racine's characters would transform any such performance into an unforgettable theatergoing experience.

Finally, let's wrap up our brief resume by mentioning another recently attempted experiment, one that has all theatergoers in mind and not just the "happy few" who know both *The Misanthrope* and *Andromache.* During a recent performance of a play we won't specify in any more detail, a certain number of ladders and stairways were set up around the stage. While reciting their lines the actors were simultaneously required to wage a fierce competition to see who among them *would climb the most steps* during the performance. The winner (not necessarily the same person each evening) received a substantial bonus; the audience could place bets, and thanks to this remarkable invention, was tempted to return for several repeat viewings!

On the night we find ourselves at the theater (it's about time we get back to the novel) a European troupe was appearing at the Poldevian Grand Theater in a performance of *Hatmel.* Since the troupe, along with a large majority of the (tourist) audience, was European, it had been decided (very much in the spirit of the previously described innovations) to multiply the roles, which would allow everyone attending to follow the play in his or her own language. There were versions offered in Poldevian and Poldadamian of course (as well as in French, English,

German, Italian, Spanish, Basque, and Welsh); the order in which the actors spoke (nine for each role) varied with every line.

Before the performance Prince Gormanskoï went backstage to have a word with the director in his dressing room. The Prince also found a tall, bald man with an intelligent, distinguished face, deeply weathered by a stormy century. He was wearing a large ripped pullover, a greenish Burberry raincoat, worn corduroy trousers and espadrilles—a blue one on his left foot, a black on his right; he had placed a copy of the day's *Times* on the makeup table, while at his feet was visible a red bag marked with "Big Shopper" (in English) from the top of which jutted a leek. He had a smile on his face. He was the great Scottish Shakespearian actor MacPrepared who had made a special trip just to play the role of Hatmel before the Prince.

Chapter 18

The Performance

The performance began with a curtain raising. But let's make sure we understand each other: all performances begin with someone or something raising a curtain, an action plainly and simply called *the* raising of *the* curtain. In the first sentence of this chapter we're not referring to this literal "raising of the curtain," an everyday occurrence hardly worth mentioning, but instead to a figurative "raising," namely, a short play that is an hors d'oeuvre of sorts to the banquet of the show, serving to whet the audience's appetite and give everybody time to get to the theater, find his seat, say hello to friends and acquaintances, and prepare for the main course: the play. The Poldevian public adores these curtain raisers; it also adores literal curtain raisings, balletlike marvels concocted by the stage crew. There's an aesthetic about curtain raisings (in the literal sense), a genuine repertoire of curtain raisings (in the literal sense) that could and already have filled volumes of criticism. This isn't what we're talking about. Our subject is "curtain raisers." Perhaps the most popular of these figurative curtain raisers, giving rise to a host of commentaries, is the following (I quote the text of the play in its entirety):

Curtain Raiser

The curtain rises.

END

The anonymous genius who authored this curtain raiser has displayed an incredible, supreme economy of means (as far as script and cast are concerned, because the staging is rather complex). It's difficult to create a work any shorter, any purer, any more dense or poignant. But yet, you'll say. . . .

But yet, indeed, how can the performance of a play entitled *Curtain Raiser,* which consists of raising a curtain, be distinguished from a (literal) curtain raising? After all, in both instances, the curtain rises. And since in *Curtain Raiser* no words are spoken. . . . "I don't see," you'll say, "how anybody can tell which one they're seeing on any given occasion." One good solution is to mention the fact in the program:

Hatmel

or "The Poldevian Tragedy"

by *Es'rhaaekpes*

with, in the role of Hatmel,
making his world debut in Poldevia
the great Scottish Shahkayspearian actor

MacPREPARED

as a curtain raiser

Curtain Raiser

by X

directed by A.V.

(in the role of the curtain,
with special permission from the Poldevian Academy,
Ph****** S******)

Seats available at: 1 Poldevian guinea, 3 Poldadamian guineas, 6 Poldevian *shlins,* 11 Poldadamian pence, 9 P. or P. farthings. Ticket office at Sainte-Gudule, left of the sacristy (ask for the beatle [name of the "beadle" in Poldevian—*translator's note*]).

But such an approach would be a rather roundabout, meta-theatrical way of going about things; and as Dr. N'Leak has irrefutably demonstrated: "There's no such thing as meta-theater."

But could you stop and think for just one minute, for Christ'smas sake! Once the curtain rises in the play *Curtain Raiser,* the play is over. Consequently, THE CURTAIN FALLS! And that's that. It rises again for *Hatmel.* Get it?

But, but, if by chance—due to some stagehand's mistake, or orders to the contrary, or some sort of delay or other (e.g., the arrival of the Reigning Prince, for instance)—if the curtain falls after having risen, how could anybody then tell that such an event is *not* a performance of the play *Curtain Raiser;* and if . . .

Enough! I said enough already! We've got other cats to skin in more ways than one (I'm sorry, Ophelia! Sorry, Alexandre Vladimirovitch! Sorry, Hotello [double sorry: Hotello hasn't appeared in the story yet]! Your nitpicking's making me write nonsense).

The curtain rose and the performance began with a curtain raiser (and don't tell me what I've just said is pleonastic or I'll quit right this second! Look at all the time we've already lost!). But this curtain raising wasn't *Curtain Raiser,* the traditional choice for special performances. This curtain raiser actually consisted of two curtain raisings. ("Were there two plays—i.e., curtain raisers—or one curtain raised twice, or two curtains raised once?" Don't ask me.)

The vast majority of curtain raisers work on the general principle of condensing plays of normal length, capable of being normally acted during a normal performance of noncurtain raisers (and we're not talking about either not raising the curtain, nor of raising a noncurtain, OK?). This creates a very warm and receptive atmosphere as a result, because the audience feels like it's getting two shows in one (in this case, three in one) for the price and length of 1.06 plays (an average curtain raiser lasts one-seventeenth of the time it takes to perform a full-length play).

So then, the audience saw:

First curtain raiser

Artaban and Atarxie

or

Suspicion (our italics)

A verse tragedy in five acts, speeded along by a few prose passages, gleaned from *Arsace* by M. Le Royer de Prade (1666).

Characters: Le Royer de Prade; Artaban, king of the Parthians; Arsace, Pharasmane, his sons; Ataraxie, daughter of the previous king; Médominie, her sister; Voronèje, the king's confidant.

Prologue.

MONSIEUR DE PRADE

The subject of this tragedy is drawn from the forty-second book of Justin in which he states that Artaban, seventh king of the Parthians, succeeded his nephew Phradalis; these few scant words contain the only kernel of truth from which the rest of the play has been spun out.

About the verse itself I shall say nothing, but those well-versed in such matters all agree that seldom have such beautifully imagined examples been encountered; they thus inspired one of the finest geniuses of our age, Monsieur Corneille, to say that he had never before seen a play so full of wit, and that it contained enough treasures to adorn three whole works.

Act I
scene 1
The scenery makes a scene.

ARTABAN

The throne I do forsake, of one mind and one heart.
My sons will rule instead; if I cling to my crown
I might well one day fall; I'd prefer to step down.

scene 2

MONSIEUR DE PRADE

Voronèje, old confidant of the King, reminds him of certain facts
which he would do well to bear in mind.

VORONÈJE

When Pharasmane was born, a subject were you still;
Arsace came next, with even greater pomp and frill;
For when the late king died, by your noble birthright
Into your hands there passed the supreme royal might.
Your sons are of one blood, but of rank unequal:
One of a monarch born, the other, a vassal;
Natural right, whether by rank or age, says the same,
That each to the future empire lays rightful claim.
Pharasmane as eldest presumes to rule alone;
Arsace, as true offspring of the man on the throne.

MONSIEUR DE PRADE

A sticky matter indeed; but the King believes he has the solution in
hand.

Enter Ataraxie.

scene 3

Scene 3. The same, plus Ataraxie, eldest daughter of the late king, therefore cousin of Artaban, who was his nephew.

THE KING

One two three four five six t'morrow you choose the man
To whom you offer the Empire, and your hand.

Artaban and Voronèje exit. Ataraxie remains alone.

scene 3b.

MONSIEUR DE PRADE

And so now you should be told that Ataraxie loves Arsace; she discusses the situation at length, at far too great a length to allow us to reproduce the results here. But what about her younger sister, Médominie?

scene 4

MÉDOMINIE [*alone*]

I love the man who, between the two, shall be king.

MONSIEUR DE PRADE

In her doubt over which of the two will be called to the empire of the Parthians she assures each man in turn of her predilection. You should be told that Arsace loves her with "dilection," Pharasmane with ambition. And in the same way that Médominie listens to the two brothers declaring their love, Pharasmane symmetrically speaks of his love to the two sisters. To Arsace, Médominie says nothing of her conversations with Pharasmane. To Pharasmane, she claims that she's deceiving Arsace and loves only him. But Pharasmane has his suspicions.

scene 5

PHARASMANE *to* MÉDOMINIE

Might you love him, Princess, though you say you don't care?

He goes off. Enter Arsace.

scene 6

ARSACE *to* MEDOMINIE

Ta ta ta ta ta ta I have come to declare
That only you can make my reign seem sweet and fair;
Ambition cannot command the flame of my heart;
I cherish most your soul, my empire's counterpart.

MONSIEUR DE PRADE

This forthright confession of love didn't sit very well at all with
Médominie, but the first act is over.

Our dual purpose in reproducing the first act here is obviously
(1) to give you some idea of the curtain-raiseration method used
by the playwright; and (2) because the subject of the play is
thematically and architecturally linked to the novel's deep
inner meaning.

In the same spirit we will limit ourselves to giving a swift
synopsis of the beginning of the second curtain raiser (just the
beginning because, as in the preceding case, telling all would
result in spilling too much and ruining the suspense):

Jealousy

by

A**** R****-G******, freeze-dried from

Jealousy Unfounded, by de Beys

102

Alindor, a friend of Bélanire, loves Clarice. Bélinire, in reality, loves Arthémise. Arthémise loves Erace. Erace loves Arthémise. Clarice is beautiful. Arthémise is beautiful. Alindor is a handsome young man, noble but poor. Belindor is rich, but noble and handsome. Erace is handsome and noble and rich. Clarice has a miserly father (but no prodigal son: she's a good girl). Arthémise is beautiful, a good girl, and free. Arthémise is Clarice's friend. Arthémise has a sister, Perside. The whole situation is very clear and very simple.

Very simply, Alindor persuades Belindor that Arthémise loves him (Perside's apparently asymmetrical role becomes understandable). He gets Erace to act like he's forsaking Arthémise and to start wooing Clarice. He persuades Clarice to pretend that she loves Erace. He persuades Arthémise to pretend that she's after Erace, but in love with Bélanire. He persuades himself that everything is going according to his plans (which are?).

But. Is Erace really pretending to be in love with Clarice? Is Clarice really pretending that she loves Erace? Is Arthémise really pretending to love Bélanire? In order to find out where things really stand, Alindor persuades Clarice to persuade Arthémise that Erace is betraying her; he persuades Arthémise to persuade Clarice that . . . etc., etc., etc., . . .

The curtain raisers having dropped curtains to the sound of thunderous applause (MacPrepared, making his world debut in the role of Alindor, was a great success), it was now time for more serious matters, i.e., *Hatmel.* Everybody knows the play so we'll limit ourselves to a brief if not blatantly compendious ("compendious" is a synonym in Old Poldevian for "brief"—*commentator's note*) description of a curious interpolation which sent a shock wave through the audience among whose notable members were M. Kosma Proutkov, the well-known Russian novelist, M. Ph****** S******, Father Risolnus, Reigning Prince Alcius and Madame ——. Suddenly, right in the middle of act 3, scene 2, interrupting the conversation between Hatmel and Ophelia, appeared a troupe of actors playing actors who started to put on *a play within a play* in the best postmodern

103

"figure in the carpet" tradition. It was a mime performance, which fact (as Father Risolnus remarked in a noisy aside) identified it as an archaic element, since the theater worked just like the movies: silents came before talkies.

Oboes. Enter the actors of the play within the play, wearing signs over their bellies: "This is the 'play within the play.'"
    Enter a King and Queen, both in love, the Queen follows close behind the King. She kneels and gives him an explicit demonstration of her love. Then he pushes her away and stretches out in a flower bed (of blue forget-me-nots). She exits. Enter a villain who swipes the King's crown, sticks it on his own head, empties the contents of a flask, marked with a skull and crossbones and the word poison *underneath, into the King's ear, then withdraws. Next, the criminal and the Queen come back together—accomplices; she kneels before him; she gives him an explicit demonstration of her love. He gives her an old Poldevian gold piece worth six guineas (a counterfeit coin, of course, since the very antique genuine articles are worth a fortune).*
    Exeunt (they exit).

The same scene was performed again but as a "talkie" the second time. And that's when the incident occurred. Reigning Prince Alcius, who didn't move a muscle during the entire mime performance, jumped to his feet and stormed out of the theater, dragging his wife Gertrude in tow. The performance went on without them.

(All commentators are still pondering to this very day, long after the event, what was behind the Reigning Prince's notice-able passivity during the performance of the first mime version of what might appear, and actually did in everyone's eyes, to be a denunciation exposing his crime [which was obviously the way he himself interpreted it, since the very next day he had his lawyers—from an American firm—file two suits against Prince Gormanskoï: (1) for defamation of character; (2) for damages on behalf of the Shahkayspear Society of America, for having plagiarized *Gone with the Wind*]. The shrewdest interpretation, which we owe to the Japanese critic Vito-Gentoushan, argued that the dumb show's lack of effect on the usurping king in *Hatmel* could be simply explained by the fact it was an interpolation, and so the actor playing the King wasn't prepared for what happened. Yet if the Reigning Prince out in the audience didn't react at first either, this wasn't because he had dozed off [all testimonies are positive: he wasn't the one snoring; the snores were coming from Father Risolnus]; nor was it because the actors were giving a bad performance [it was very good]; no, it was quite simply because *nothing had been told:* what is shown without being told doesn't count; what counts is what's told; it doesn't matter if you show what's supposed to be kept silent and not told. By contrast, when the same scene was performed again, *with sound,* he could no longer ignore it and remain calmly in his seat as though nothing were going on.)

Part Four

*Perhaps You Were Hoping for
a Graceful Return to Days of Yore?*

Chapter 19

A Rough End to the Year

The day after the big scandal at the *Hatmel* performance in the National Theater of Eërlosni Castle, Father Risolnus, now acting prime minister after Poldevius's assassination, summoned Prince Gormanskoï to his office. He had ordered up several freshly tapped kegs of beer so as to be ready for anything that might come his way; he had his office made over into a pub, with the ministry's ushers drawing his pints of draft. After handing the Prince an offprint of his latest refutation of the indefensible theses ("whose meaning is unconstruable," to quote precisely his conclusion) propounded by his enemy in theory, Louis Macaniche, he explained the reason for the summons.

"My dear Prince, I have been commissioned by the Reigning Prince to deliver these orders into your hands."

The Prince took, opened, read, thanked, left.

"Fine," Father Risolnus thought, "that's one down." He consulted his appointment schedule. He had a meeting with Misters T. and T.

"Show them in," he said to the usher, "and pour me a Guinness."

Misters T. and T. entered.

"My dear Misters T. and T., I have been commissioned by the Reigning Prince to deliver these orders into your hands: to whom do I give them?"

"Me," said T.

"Me," said T' (T' refers to a duplicate copy of T.).

"No big deal!" Father Risolnus said. He pulled a second

copy of the orders out of his pocket. Then he shut his eyes to keep from finding out who took which; it was too early in the morning for exercises in logic. Misters T. and T. took the orders and left.

All this activity made Father Risolnus work up a thirst and reinflamed his tennis elbow. He decided to call it quits for the day, go home, plop down on his bed with a drink in his hand and a good book of gobbledygook ("gobbledygook" is a synonym for "metaphysics" in Father Risolnus's language game—*note by the official exegete of the Poldevian Hexarchy*).

After leaving the ministry Prince Gormanskoï went to the airport and took the first plane out for Le Havre. He was holding a passport issued to a certain Thehatmel.

After leaving the office, Misters T. and T. went to the airport and presented themselves at the check-in counter for the first Poldevian Airlines flight out to Le Havre. The clerk, a woman from Normandy by the name of Jeanne Semoule, took their tickets; they had been issued to a certain Mr. Tweedledum, Esquire, and Tweedledee, Esquire. Jeanne hesitated. She wanted to know which one was Mr. Tweedledum, and which Mr. Tweedledee, in order to give each his appropriate boarding pass. But she knew there was no point in asking them who was who because they didn't always tell the truth. Ever since Mr. Raymond Smullyan reported his research findings in the book entitled *What Is the Title of This Book?*, it was a known fact that one member of the pair lied on Mondays, Tuesdays, and Wednesdays, and told the truth the other days of the week (in Poldevia there are 6 + 1 days in a week). His brother lied on Thursdays, Fridays, and Saturdays, telling the truth on the other days. "What day's today?" Jeanne Semoule wondered. She had forgotten. No big deal. Addressing Misters T. and T. together, she said: "When do you lie?"

"I lie on Saturdays and I lie on Sundays," one answered.

"I lie tomorrow," the other answered.

"In that case," Mademoiselle Semoule went on, "which one

of you is Tweedledum?"

"I'm Tweedledum," one said.

"If that's true, then I'm Tweedledee."

"All right," Jeanne said with relief; and she handed each his boarding pass.

Prince Gormanskoï, alias Thehatmel, was strolling through the streets of Le Havre, and he didn't care one bit for what he saw. But he was far more unhappy with himself than with any scenery: had he done the right thing by accepting this proposed mission that had traps at every turn? Did he really have to go through with this narrative sequence and continue to mimic the movements of an ancient story in the hope of untangling the threads of his own? That was the problem, that was the question: "To be or not to be Hatmel, etc.," he thought. Plus, he was in an awful hurry, given Hortense's abduction, and he didn't have time to relive that messy saga! After getting off at the trolley stop where a little girl had arranged to meet him at her sister's that evening, his steps imperceptibly led him to the Delacolline Bookstore.

Lit by dazzling halogen lamps the Delacolline Bookstore flooded with brightness the short stretch of Avenue Boris Vian, blazing brilliantly like an Argus with its hundred piercing eyes. Up close you might have thought it was some supermarket specializing in detergent and clothespins, but it was in reality a "sanctuary for intelligence, culture, and civilization." In the dazzling halogen lamplight the Delacolline Bookstore sold to the countless book lovers of this metropolis a whole panoply of indispensable volumes, ranging from the works of Madame Zaraï to those of Ph****** S******.

(We've now reached the midpoint of the novel, a fact we need to bring to your attention: ever since the story started we have been scaling the slope of mysteries, climbing the steep, riddle-strewn slope; and now we've arrived at the top.

Soon, in less than a few lines, we are going to start our downward journey toward the plain, still off in the distant mists, through which flows the majestic calm waters of the river called END. And when we reach its banks, in the last chapter, we will understand everything, we will know everything; or just about. For perhaps even then, on the other side of the river, through yet other mists a vague shape will loom, like the white cliffs of Dover seen from an approaching Hovercraft: the land of a sequel, of a new series of adventures; who knows?)

Once inside the bookstore, Gormanskoï-Thehatmel asked for the person he was supposed to meet, M. Frédéric. But the manager informed him that, alas, M. Frédéric had just been arrested for espionage: he was suspected of having facilitated the export to foreign powers, in particular to P—— and P——, of precious cutting-edge technologies that permitted any country to replace the nontransmission of information and opinions by a single TV channel with the free transmission of an unvarying stock of the same information and opinions by an unlimited number of channels under different names. "His case is serious, Monsieur Thehatmel," the manager said. M. Thehatmel agreed. The director took this opportunity to sell him an under-the-counter copy of the *Critique of Pure Reason* which had just been withdrawn from the market following Mr. Kant's conviction for plagiarism (because he had disgracefully copied the work of a great American philosopher, Margaret Mitchell).

On leaving the bookstore he headed toward a movie house in the center of town to kill the necessary time before his date with the big sister of the little girl whom he had met on the trolley (only Poldevian princes have little girls setting up dates for them with their big sisters). He picked out a movie house with a long and especially boring feature (he needed to get some sleep): *Gone with* (no, no, no, no, no, no, they weren't playing *Gone with;* enough already, it's a genuine obsession, good God; and as for the comic effect of repetition, that works for a while, but then it wears thin). I'll start over: the movie house he chose was playing a long and especially boring film, or a boring and especially long film, or a not so long but especially boring film, take your pick: *The L*** E*******, for example, or *Cle*******. But certainly not *The Princess Bride*.

When he came out it was dark; a steady rain was falling on Le Havre. The Prince hurried along through the dark slick streets shifting with ever infrequent shadows. And among these shifting shadows, by the Prince unsuspected, by the Prince undetected, were those of Tweedledum and Tweedledee, the Reigning Prince's hired killers who had been quite literally *shadowing* him. One (Tweedledum?) shadowed him from behind; and the other (Tweedledee?) from the front. Now everybody knows how to shadow a person from behind, but shadowing someone from the front takes some special doing! And the Prince, who suspected nothing, continued his conversation with himself: "If I must be Hatmel, I will be my own kind of Hatmel, not the one I'm forced to be. Therefore: to be or not to be Hatmel, that's the real question."

Chapter 20

Ophelia Lets Herself Be Persuaded

Take your book and turn to the beginning of Chapter 13. In order to get to Chapter 13 you have several algorithms at your disposal to program on your personal computer.

For a clearer idea, let's take a look at two examples: Algorithm A and Algorithm B (the word *algorithm* is said to come from the Persian, a transformation of the last part of the name Abu Ja'far Mohammed ibn Musa al-Khuwarizmi-Mollah-het, at first producing "algorithmaimolette," then ultimately simplified to its final form: "algorithm." Father Risolnus maintains that the word should in fact be read as "algorhythm" from "algo" and "rhythm" [the Spanish word *algo* means "something," hence "something about rhythm"], but no other author subscribes to this idea.

Algorithm A, or the "algorithm for searching in sequence," entails stockpiling in your memory a list of all the successive word-pairs in the novel in their order of appearance; each pair is placed in numerical order. Algorithm A sets about searching for these words one by one in your memory list, and replacing them. The algorithm tests every pair it finds by comparing it to the phrase "Chapter 13"; if the results are positive, the computer flashes the sequence number it has reached and stops; now all you have to do is turn to the indicated place. If it doesn't ever find "Chapter 13," which happens for instance in those novels left in American hotel rooms, after running through the entire list, it flashes a "0" and goes off to lunch. But that isn't the case here. This algorithm is infallible (unless you yourself have forgotten to input the word-pair "Chapter 13"), but it eats up a lot of time. Let's move on to Algorithm B.

It works on a simple principle as well: you start out by capturing the word-pairs in alphabetical order as in a dictionary. Then they're numbered in sequence. But instead of testing them one at a time, you skip to the *middle* of the list. If the pair you're looking for comes after the middle row the search starts all over again, but only after erasing the first half of the list; in the opposite case, it's the second half of the list that's eliminated. You begin again in the same way, by splitting the remaining chunk in half; you reach the result very quickly. Rigorous demonstrations have shown that Algorithm B is always faster than Algorithm A, whenever the novel contains more than thirty-seven words. Such is the case at present. (Professor Knoutdzoï of the Poldevian Institute for Programming claims that hexachotomic division [by 6] is more efficient than the dichotomic division used by Algorithm B; we leave him all responsibility for this statement.)

At any rate, whichever algorithm you prefer, turn to Chapter 13 (it has been brought to my attention that since the novel has a table of contents, there exists a third algorithm that could do the job: Algorithm C. According to my correspondent, Algorithm C takes the list of chapters found in the table and then applies either Algorithm A or Algorithm B according to the same procedures, but *just on this list,* far shorter (always shorter by its very nature, he maintains; but I still haven't verified this crucial assertion); then you turn to the corresponding page whose number is indicated by the table).

(A little later: Algorithm C does indeed seem faster than the first two. However when it comes to searching for Chapter 13 in the table of contents it's hard to choose between Algorithm A and Algorithm B, because there are thirty-seven chapters and thirty-seven is exactly the number at which both algorithms average the same working speed; this fact, passed over by our correspondent M. Inchtin, somewhat reduces the general import of his discovery. But there's an even more serious problem: **at least one case exists in which it is false that the table of contents list is shorter than the others;** namely, in the novel by my friend Denis Duabuor. I give the text in its entirety [omitting only the table of contents that can be easily deduced].

Denis Duabuor

Thirty-Seven Chapters

A Novel

In this case the table of contents method is in fact a little longer than the two others. Nevertheless I do thank M. Inchtin for his interesting suggestions.)

So here we are back at the beginning of Chapter 13 just at the moment when the eyes of the characters gathered in the kitchen —Laurie, Carlotta, Jim Wedderburn—turn toward Ophelia, who is perusing Hortense's letter of distress.

Ophelia turns pale under her fur and meows plaintively: "No," she says, "please! I don't want to go to Poldevia; I don't want to drown in Hortense's place; I don't want to get caught in my garland of daisies and nettles on some willow branch over a stream; I don't want the branch to break; I don't want to fall into the weeping brook and sink under the weight of my wet fur in the stream while singing myself to my muddy death! No! Please!"

"Is she crazy?" Carlotta asked Laurie.

"She's understood what we expect from her," Jim Wedderburn said, "we want her to be Hortense's understudy. *Comment qu'on dit en francais:* 'understudy'?"

"We say *doublure,* meaning 'double' or 'dubber'; but we definitely don't say '*comment qu'on dit en francais*' no more than we say '*quelle heure qu'il est.*' "

"Did anybody hear me say '*quelle heure qu'il est?*' " Jim Wedderburn said, "*la joue* of that girl!"

"What about my 'cheek'? Oh, I give up," Carlotta said.

"What's happening," Laurie said, "is that they want to force her Prince into playing the role of Hamlet in a Poldevian tragedy of princely succession or something along those lines; unless it's the Prince himself who's got this idea, it's not clear, but somebody's got to keep Hortense from meeting the same fate which lays in store for Hamlet's fiancée in the play, whose name—let me remind you—is Ophelia. Our very own Ophelia has only just now remembered how her namesake dies in Shakespeare's version of the scene. But we can't have any of that, we can't have any of that at all; nobody's sending our little pet out somewhere to get herself drowned. No way! Poor little thing."

"Nobody's going to do that to my pussycat, no!" Carlotta cried, hitting a more hysterical note.

"Meow!" Ophelia said, leaping onto Laurie's shoulder and giving her a kiss on her muzzle; then Ophelia did the same with Carlotta.

"Ophelia! You stink!" Laurie said.

Jim Wedderburn then explained that this didn't in any way involve putting Ophelia in danger; she would replace Hortense for only as long as it took to unravel the plot; but she wasn't running any risks because Hortense was the person targeted insofar as she was Gormanskoi's fiancée, not Ophelia who, in the equation Gormanskoi=Hamlet, was a fiancée in name only; and that was precisely the reason he had thought of her.

"Who's this 'he'?"

"But you know," Jim Wedderburn whispered in Laurie's ear. "Come on now, let's not get thrown off the track by any unbridled nominalism!" he concluded. And what's more, Ophelia wasn't the least bit in love with the Prince, she loved only Carlotta (first) and Laurie (second).

The negotiations were long and heated. Ophelia demanded guarantees to be paid in advance in the form of smoked salmon and glazed chestnuts (one of her favorite dishes). Jim Wedderburn promised to go to Fortnum and Mason's on his next trip to London and bring back some "brandy butter"; also, to travel with her to Poldevia. In short, Ophelia was bargaining from a position of strength and she used it to her full advantage.

"OK," Laurie said, "we'll send her, but for no more than a week."

"That's a promise," Jim Wedderburn said.

"But it just now occurs to me," Carlotta said, "are you sure she'll know how to play her role? As far as the innocence act goes, she'll be fine, she's an expert; but what will people say if they catch Shakespeare's Ophelia redhanded as she's swiping salmon from the kitchen after dinner?"

Ophelia promised to control herself.

Chapter 21

Notebook of a Return to the Land of My Birth

The day after the day after the day before saw Ophelia set out for Poldevia. She left to help Hortense, accompanied by Jim Wedderburn, a young man whom she trusted somewhat: he had a long, level, comfortable lap; he wouldn't forget to feed her; he'd hold her paw whenever she felt any momentary depression over being so far from Laurie and Carlotta.

The day before the trip Carlotta and she got her things together: these included her favorite cushion, her red dish, her Ping-Pong ball, a ball of yarn that matched the color of her fur, one or two emergency cans of cat food, her Kleenex, vitamins, a deck of cards for playing Patience, and a notebook for her impressions. Ophelia had spent her childhood in Poldevia, and she retained vague, happy images of those days despite the tragedy at Lake Melankton (see *Hortense in Exile*, Chapter 14). Who knows whether she'll be able to locate traces of her parents? She wanted to get to the bottom of it all and maybe, one day, publish her memoirs which she planned on calling *Notebook of a Return to the Land of My Birth*.

So this morning she opened the door for Jim Wedderburn at the crack of dawn, found a place in her basket, and off they went to the —— train station from which the Trans-Europ Express, *The Poldevian*, departed. She had demanded, and obtained (disgracefully exploiting the situation) a first-class seat in a Corail train, because that way she'd be able to nestle on the baggage rack under the carriage roof and explore her surroundings at her leisure.

119

Our travelers arrived with a comfortable margin before the scheduled departure time (this wasn't exactly what Jim Wedderburn would have preferred, but during extraordinary circumstances a person's got to know how to take extraordinary risks. Following his grandfather's advice, Reverend Timothy M., Jim Wedderburn never broke the golden rule of train travel: **"You must arrive at a train station in time to miss the preceding train."** Ophelia and Carlotta had no objections, but changed their minds when Laurie [who always caught her trains with at most + or − six seconds to spare] pointed out that there was only one train a day for Poldevia, which left at 8:37 A.M., and that [1] their journey would inevitably be delayed until the next day, which was serious, given how swiftly events were unfolding; and [2] they would have to wait almost twenty-four hours in the station. It was the second point that clinched the argument for Ophelia).

They settled in their seats, unfolded their newspapers (the *Times* for Jim Wedderburn, *Cat World* for Ophelia), and waited. Soon a voice announced out on the platform:

"The train for Queneau'stown will leave on track no. 6. There will be stops at:

Alright
Anyoldton
Ardvark
Atall
Attenshun
*Ball
Baccarat
*Bald Heights
Bangher—with shuttle-bus service to Banghim
*Barrel
Bayouhoo
*Beaumont-on-Herring
Beavervue
Belchville

Bemine
*Bergburg
Bigbird
Bigjam
Bigmess
Bison
*Bleary
Boondocksboro
Buggerburg—with shuttle-bus service to Bughausen
Butts Gap
*Byebyeford

. . . .

Ohnooo
Oneuptown
Onnion
Orange
Orgone
Osmosis
Oshun
Ovary

. . . .

Quaitasec
Qawshun

. . . .

Queneau'stown
Connections at Ball for Catawbaha.
Connections at Bald Heights for Catamice, Catbaret.
Connections at Barrel for Cat Ballou, Catboose, Catchacha.
Connections at Beaumont-on-Herring for Catchatory, Catch-ferayze, Catch 22, Catchup, Catheeze, Cathodes.
Connections at Bergburg for Catklizm, Catlick, Catlogs, Catnmouz, Catonsville, Catracks, Catscan, Catskalls, Catskills.
Connections at Bleary for Catstrophy, Cattarauguts, Cattaver, Catzaway, Ceal, Ceelion, Ceewanee, Cheeiit, Chalay, Chalotte, Chashay.

Connections at Byebyeford for Coan, Cohen, Condom, Condummintz, Conjob, Corps-Knee, Croutons, Cucuron, Cudos, Cumquat, Cungfoolz, Cunterfits, Cuntervue, Dewkatz.

. . . .

Stand clear of the doors!"

They traveled all through the day, they traveled all through the night; the scenery flashed by; the train stopped at its stops, then left again; some travelers got off, others got on. Ophelia and Jim Wedderburn chatted, snored, drank, ate, pissed, slept, awoke, played War, whist, "Seven and a Half," Kings, go, watched the cows pass by, counted the telegraph poles, calculated how fast the train was going, checked the schedule; in short, it was your average train trip!

Every now and then Ophelia climbed down from her baggage rack, took her cat credit card from her belongings and went out to phone Carlotta and/or Laurie. The Trans-Europ Express, *The Poldevian,* at the cutting edge of progress, places at the disposal of its travelers a phone booth from which you can actually make calls! You step in, unhook the receiver, slip in your credit card, dial your number and talk. No matter that you've been racing away from your phone friend at three hundred kilometers an hour, he'll still be on the line; it's just incredible! "Meow, purr, purr, meow," Ophelia said into the phone, her eyes on the dial racking up the message units at a speed proportional to the train's.

They crossed borders. Customs and police officers moved through the train, asked for passports, ID cards, family record books. The ticket collectors collected tickets. There were plains, there were mountains, there were snows that were eternal and others less permanent. In a small, dark station, around two in the morning, a voice on a platform shouted through the mist and darkness: "Beer, sandwiches, white wine, red whiiine!" It stirred the emotions.

At last people started to shake themselves off, pat their cheeks, rub their eyes, put their clothes back on, take down

suitcases, grow restless. Jim Wedderburn and Ophelia got their
things together calmly, displaying the steady composure of
seasoned veterans of long international journeys. Ophelia got
back into her basket. The train stopped at the next-to-last
station: Lake Melankton. They got off. On the platform awaiting them were Inspectors Blognard and Arapède.

It would indeed have been too dangerous to go to the end of
the line, all the way into Queneau'stown itself: it would have
come down to throwing themselves into the wolf's jaws, i.e.,
into the hands of the Reigning Prince's agents. Instead they
would go to the same hotel where the Blognards and the
Arapèdes had put up, then review the situation. Ophelia went
right to her room (with balcony and lake view—she shared a
suite with Jim Wedderburn), unhooked the receiver (room
service: 14) and ordered Norwegian salmon with blinis; then
she called Carlotta. Two hours later she went down to the hotel
lounge to rejoin her companions.

At this time of day you could find a good dozen or so hotel
clients seated on black, drably cushioned garden chairs at the
outdoor tables. Toward the outer rim three or four Poldadamian
gentlemen were slumped in sleep; their faces, baked crimson by
the infrared action of whiskey, declared their hereditary haughti-
ness. They were accompanied by dull governesses and wives in
hat veils. In the distance was also a pair of lovers, flanked by a
particularly pesky, dimwitted pointer who constantly hankered
for some loving attention. As one witness wrote: "In order to
kiss, the couple had to dodge the dog continually, push him
aside, fight their way into a nondog world." With a deft flick of
her claw Ophelia set the situation right. Just then, a female cat
with red fur walked into the room. Ophelia looked at her and
was swept by an intense wave of nostalgia. "Mommy!" she
meowed. "My daughter," the other echo-meowed in response.

Ophelia's mother was named Tioutcha; in her youth she had
been a "purring slave" for the great philosopher Orsells, from
whose home she had been banished when her sinful affair with

123

Alexandre Vladimirovitch was discovered. From their union Ophelia was born. Having herself escaped the pirates who had kittennapped her daughter, she long despaired of ever laying eyes on Ophelia again. However, her presence in this hotel was a pure accident. For some time now she had known that her daughter was safe and sound and happy (how? we'll find out in due course); and so she had rushed over to meet her. Mother and daughter had endless matters to catch up on and so we'll give them some privacy for their cat-chat.

That very evening Alexandre Vladimirovitch came over to visit them in their room on his way back to the City. "Hello, dear daughter," he said; and he lavished his love upon her with a kiss. He lavished so much love upon her in fact that Ophelia felt obliged to point out that the incestuous relationship he seemed to have in mind was completely out of the question. Carlotta had arranged Ophelia's engagement and eventual marriage of convenience with an excellent cat by the name of Leonskoï; but Leonskoï had been poisoned; and Ophelia, choosing to remain celibate for the rest of her life, had sworn that henceforth she would love only Laurie and Carlotta. Alexandre Vladimirovitch, who had shown himself polite in making his proposal of incest, bowed to her wishes. Everybody knows that cats keep incest in the family (as we human beings do ourselves in those increasingly hard-to-find corners of our society, still unperverted by the modern world, where a sense of community has survived intact). This is one reason for the exceptional virtuosity of their genetic combinations, since their kinship networks are extremely complex. The incest taboo, pride of the human race, has marked human family trees with a great recursive banality. By contrast you would need the full power of a Turing machine to untangle the skein of blood ties between Alexandre Vladimirovitch and Tutankhamen, for example, calculations the least cat can compute in less time than it takes to swallow a canary.

Alexandre Vladimirovitch caught Ophelia up on the situation's latest developments and the role she would need to play. "My daughter, I'm counting on you; what's bred in the bone will come out in the flesh. Meow!"

Chapter 22

Hortense Is Rescued

Everything is inexorably falling into place; the Wheel of Fortune is still spinning at the great Fair of the Throne of the Universe, with one notch to go before stopping. Which is a way of saying what? Hortense is a prisoner of Prince Augre; Prince Augre has breathed life into an emanation of his lechery, with Hortense as its vector; in other words, into a living statue, a doll made of flesh: the Fake Hortense. Prince Airt'n, or Gormanskoï, is in Hamletian exile in Le Havre. Alexandre Vladimirovitch, reunited with his daughter Ophelia, is off to Laurie and Carlotta's in the City. Everything is falling into place: Fate! *forza del destino!* Hortense must be rescued; she is in dire need of rescue! Hortense's rescue is the critical question of the hour, a coming-to-a-head of necessity. But who, aided by Cyrandzoï, the Pony Prince, was going to rescue Hortense? A prince, none other than a prince, and only one possible prince at that: Gormanskoï's "brother," his alter ego, his double, Prince Acrab'm.

It's almost midnight. His head covered in a green hood, Acrab'm swam across the dark moat to the foot of the stairs leading to the door which opens on the room where Augre's henchmen are keeping watch. Hortense is being held prisoner in the second room whose window no longer looks out on the tube diabolically positioned to engulf Hortense in the oubliettes of Zenda, but directly onto the black water of the moat and the waiting arms of Acrab'm, warm and snug in his green frog-Prince wet suit, hooded in incognito green. Any moment now Cyrandzoï is going to launch the attack.

And what has Augre been up to all this time? Why doesn't he

come back and harass Hortense with his insistent pleas? *Fatalitas! Fatalitas!* In the arms of the Fake Hortense he has forgotten her! With the Fake Hortense, in her false flesh practically indistinguishable from the real thing, he has been wallowing in every illicit variation his imagination can concoct, fueled by his book and videotape library. And the Fake Hortense, already insanely jealous of Hortense, eggs him on; she tries to outdo him with her perverted acrobatics, her lascivious intercontortions; she performs the "corkscrew" (?), the "hunting horn" (??) on him; she offers herself "Romorantin" style, à la papa, à la pope, à la popo (???), who can count the ways? And she talks to him, she whispers, she roars, she coos, she lashes him with obscenities, she "ah my Augre!"'s him, she "do this" and "do that"'s him, she "that again, right here again, again"'s him. She burns the guy out, revives him, sucks him dry, she turns his brain to oatmeal. In short, he's not going to be in any position to spring into action.

And so absolutely everything's in place. Midnight begins to toll. Cyrandzoï charges the door. As it starts to give way a fiendishly loud alarm is triggered throughout the underground network; but Augre doesn't react; the Fake Hortense stops up his ears with new propositions (yes, another proposition . . .). The door gives way. The henchmen put up a fight. One charges into the second room, grabs Hortense, and shoves her into what he thinks is the tube. Hortense falls; she figures she's done for now; she faints; she splashes into the dark waters of the moat; but Acrab'm grabs hold of her. The Prince swims off; he crosses the ditch with our beautiful Hortense in his arms like a gift package. How beautiful she is! How lucky Gormanskoï is! Her nightie opens; he closes it again; pull yourself together, Acrab'm; go on, hide that breast, it's not for your eyes; Hortense, you're beautiful! Cyrandzoï knocks out the henchmen with a few uppercuts with his pony-shoes (plus a few jabs for good measure). Prince Augre staggers onto the scene, his face pale; too late! With infinite care Acrab'm places the precious package (Hortense in a swoon) across Cyrandzoï's croup. He pulls his green hood back down; zips his frog-Prince suit back up; clings to the Pony Prince's mane. They're off and running with a vengeance, they fly along, and swim, and even do a bit of jumping. Finally they set foot on the shore of Lake Melankton. The moon is shining bright. The moon, beautiful, redheaded, indifferent, rose upon the whole scene, upon the vast array of human dramas; she climbed through the sky, casting a long, sleepy gaze down upon Space, Mystery, the Abyss, and for a brief moment the eyes of the shining lady and the suffering Prince met.

The Wheel of Fortune came to a dead stop. Everything is completely and fatally in place. Hortense wakes up; the Prince lifts his hood, an unruly lock of his beautiful hair falls down his face. "You!" Hortense says. "You at last! Dear God, thank you!" She kisses him. "Oh, such a beautiful hood," she whispers, "such a beautiful red hood!"

Chapter 23

The Downfall

It was one morning a short while later, New Year's morning in Poldevia. Father Risolnus was listening to his favorite choral work: *The Old Year Has Come and Gone.* The parties were over, and we ducked out of them all; whew!

The new year had arrived with all its pagan fervor. In Poldevia as elsewhere, paganism is the perpetually reflowering fruit of the turning seasons. The air was mild, with a touch of spring.

(Hortense's diary) Rescued at last, and it was about time, too. I practically drowned when they threw me down that ridiculous tube. Gormanskoï looked so proud of himself that I didn't dare complain. But he didn't even come up and sleep by my side. I'm actually rather happy to have a room all to myself; even if it's not really like being at home. It's true, I'm starting to miss the City; sure, there are a few good bookstores here, but what a pain to have to keep your eyes glued to your feet so you won't disturb any snails. Plus all these ponies! They're absolutely insolent; and so cantankerous. It's almost nice out today. . . .

Hortense was waiting for the Prince in his apartments. Yes, Hortense was waiting for the Prince, but she thought she was waiting for **the** Prince, but instead **a** Prince, who wasn't **the** Prince, showed up.

During her midnight rescue Hortense had taken the Prince for *the* Prince, and the Prince never set her straight. Why not? His answer to this question is categorical and can't be challenged: he *wasn't able to do so,* he was forbidden. Prince Gormanskoï was in Le Havre, which Hortense didn't know; but then she **wasn't supposed to know.** The most absolute secrecy was imperative; she wasn't supposed to know a thing about the pitched go match (at the sixth *dan* level at least) being played between the Reigning Prince's forces and those of the Premier Presumed Prince.

For Ophelia was now ready to get down to work, to "atari" (the equivalent of the expression "checkmate" in go) the attempt to get rid of Hortense by drowning (or, failing that, by pneumonia). Hortense had to be kept completely out of the way. Therefore the Prince wasn't able to tell Hortense the truth. He saw her every day, phoned her, responded ambiguously to her remarks, which now and then made him blush. The latter was easier than it sounds because Gormanskoï's standoffishness toward his fiancée before her abduction (an attitude whose cause she now understood would surely disappear, thanks to his friends) had gotten her used to his dispassion both in words and concrete deeds. Yet . . . however. . . .

For was Prince Acrab'm mindful enough? Did he really do everything necessary to keep Hortense looking forward to a brighter, more loving future? Did Hortense's growing flame of passion, evident both in what she said and hoped for, have no connection whatsoever to his own actions? I wonder now. He sent Hortense flowers. All right. He visited her five or six times a day, always accompanied by Cyrandzoï who just loved taking baths in the big tub. All right again. He sent her poems, by definition love poems, since he was, after all, **the** Prince's stand-in.

"Stand-in": both the linguistic structure and implications of this expression tortured him: for we should just come out and say that **Prince Acrab'm was in love with Hortense!** It took nothing at all—a split-second glimpse of the tip of her nipple in the moonlight—for love's arrow (generally shot from the eyes, but there are exceptions), unwittingly released by Hortense's breast, to pierce him through; ever since then it remained embedded in his heart like an intractable barb and set it on fire. Thus when he sent her some poems under his assumed name of Gormanskoï, the poems also spoke indirectly for himself; take this sonnet as an example:

Sonnet, FOR HORTENSE

I send the report, today updated,
Of my heart's torment for this week;
Tears, belly growls, sighs, cries, phlegm, muscle tweaks,
Each tells true how my soul is afflicted;
Counting the ways your cruel heart inflicted
Such torture strikes me all of a heap;
When evening comes I take refuge in sleep
From side effects that can't be avoided.
Alas! if seeing them, with eyes moistened
You won't feel I am to be pitied
And answer right away (by Chronopost)
That you promise me of all gifts the best
One choice will I have (my life now lost):
Fall out of my bed to eternal rest.

Hortense thought the poem was nerdy; and she was right. But maybe she ought to have paid more attention to the oddness of the occurrence; and so, by means of this subtle transition, we shift our focus to Hortense. How could Hortense have failed to realize that the Prince wasn't *the* Prince? That standing before her eyes was Acrab'm, and consequently not Gormanskoï? On that first night when she got rescued, all right, that's understandable, but what about later? Shouldn't she have been suspicious? When something looks odd, like the Prince's fit of sonnet-composing nerdiness, it means that something *is* odd; and when I say "odd," I mean it was strange indeed: Gormanskoï had never composed a sonnet in his life.

But here's what happened: Acrab'm was Gormanskoï's identical twin; and Hortense's previously developed sensitivity

131

to the difference between good and evil was of no use here: Acrab'm was good, he was Gormanskoï's friend, his brother, his "alter ego." You'll say that Hortense had already been through a princely mix-up on first meeting Augre; and she knew about Acrab'm's existence, wasn't surprised she hadn't heard from him, and so she asked him for news of himself without knowing it was him; her past experience ought to have sparked her suspicions. Yes, but there's only one problem: experience is good for nothing; it teaches us how to behave in circumstances like those that have already occurred, not in totally unfamiliar situations. Experience in life and in physics are two different things. When somebody tells you, or you say to yourself: "experience has taught me . . .," ask that person, or yourself, the following question: "Taught what?" The only sound you'll hear is silence.

Where's this story going? We're worried.

Hortense was waiting; the Prince was due to arrive. But on this particular day Hortense was waiting in her bathtub! And why not? If the Prince wanted to keep up his show of indifference, so much the worse; otherwise, so much the better (so she thought). Except that there were a few things she didn't know; and Alexandre Vladimirovitch wasn't on the rim of the tub like some Jiminy Cricket (synonym for "moral conscience"—*Commentator's note*). We're getting more and more worried.

So then let's continue our description of Hortense taking her bath, already twice interrupted (Chapters 1 and 15): forsaking her breasts, her soapy hand moved down toward her belly; first she scrubbed insistently, meticulously and fondlingly her very round navel; then she dropped even lower, pensively grazing that soft, downy zone whose colorless fuzz was set on either side of a line running down the middle, symmetrical to the one along her back, as strong and healthy as a hare's (a sign of great beauty, according to the troubadour Bertran de Born), all the way down to where her (perfect) buttocks parted. This was followed by another zone, more often than not skimpily concealed by a pair of panties, which we can refer to as her private tuft, a soft shade of light brown verging on blonde. Her hand, still dreamy (we say "hand" instead of Hortense; it's Hortense who's "dreamy"; her hand's busy soaping), clutched and completely covered it with her solid, silken, sturdy grasp. She quivered. She soaped herself more slowly, moving counter-clockwise; then a little more quickly. She quivered again; sighed; and her finger . . .

At that precise instant the door opened and the Prince appeared; she turned her beautiful, slightly misty eyes toward him, with her lips parted: "Ah," she said; and what was fatally, catastrophically destined to happen, happened. She showed him in and in he came.

Let's skip backwards in time again: another morning, the first of the year in Le Havre. Prince Gormanskoï was off to his date with big Madeleine, the sister of the little girl he had met on the trolley. His "guardian angels," Misters T. and T., kept shadowing him. As he turned onto Avenue Raymond Queneau, from the third story window of a shady, suspicious-looking establishment, the Bouvard and Pécuchet Hotel, a naked woman signaled to him. He looked up: it was Hortense!

Chapter 24

The Downfall

The fact that Chapter 24 shares an identical title with Chapter 23 signals their parallel relationship. And it's no accident that Gormanskoï glancing up at the window of the Bouvard and Pécuchet Hotel and **seeing** Hortense parallels Hortense glancing up at her rescuer on the shores of Lake Melankton and **seeing** Gormanskoï. Such a signal "signifies," as we say nowadays. An inescapable logic of cataclysmic confusion runs through the whole situation, reminding us of the primordial, archaic, and telluric nature of all beginnings, best expressed by the equally archaic poetic figure of parallelism. "If it's parallel," Louis Macaniche remarks, "then it's not perpendicular."

Let's expand on this.

First of all, is it possible for Hortense to be actually present in the flesh and nothing but the flesh, at the Bouvard and Pécuchet Hotel in Le Havre on this January morning? No: at this very same instant she is in her tub in Poldevia, making ready to welcome the Prince who isn't *the* Prince, since *the* Prince is in Le Havre on Avenue Raymond Queneau. Hortense doesn't have the gift of being everywhere at once (*Cf.* Father Risolnus: "On Being in the Same Place at the Same Time: A Problem in Hortensian Studies," *Journal of Poldevian Metaphysics* 69.6: 35-53.). Consequently the woman signaling to Gormanskoï from the window isn't Hortense; she looks so much like Hortense that Gormanskoï takes her for Hortense; she possesses the charming Hortensian characteristic of parading stark naked around her bedroom, but *she isn't Hortense;* at the very best she's a Canada Dry Hortense. Who is she? If not Hortense, might she be a fake Hortense? Right on the button! She's the Fake Hortense.

When Augre, the Demon Prince, arriving on the scene too late, saw the condition to which Cyrandzoï's pony-shoes had reduced his henchmen; then rushing into Hortense's prison, also saw that Hortense had flown the coop along with the bird (the Prince had birdnapped a robin redbreast, also rescued by Cyrandzoï), his first impulse was to throw in the towel; but he quickly got hold of himself. His powerful intellect, although weakened by sextraordinary hours spent in the Fake Hortense's company, had just concocted a new scheme. You get one guess.

"Darling, how did you get here?" the Prince asked with surprise (he was now inside the bedroom). "Who told you?"

"Your brother, Prince Acrab'm; he was the one who rescued me; he didn't want to reveal the secret but I persuaded him," the Fake Hortense said with a suggestive glance, trying (in obedience to her instructions) to insinuate as much as possible with one single look.

This irresponsible breach of security made Prince Gormanskoï frown, but he didn't seem to catch the implications of the Fake Hortense's eyes. His trust in his brother was unshakable; the slightest **suspicion** couldn't even cross his mind (kindly note the use of this word, moreover printed in boldface— *Narrator's note*).

"But aren't you happy to see me, my love?" the saucy wench simpered, pretending to hide her breasts and pubic hair out of modesty, but actually throwing her buttocks out behind her and turning her body in such a way that Gormanskoï couldn't keep his eyes off her. "Tell me, my little Prince, tell me that you forgive your Hortense; I missed you like crazy!"

The Prince's eyes filled in spite of themselves with those deceptive (but there was no way he could know!) Hortensian charms. The already lengthy period of chastity made mandatory by the traditional Poldevian rules governing vendettas, due to continue until his father's death was avenged and the Reigning

Prince punished, began to weigh upon him heavily. Furthermore, he was far from Poldevia; and Alexandre Vladimirovitch, that most steadfast guardian of traditions, wasn't around; nobody would find out about his slight bending of the rules. He became a different person; the Gormanskoï of yesteryear reappeared, turning back into the man he had been during those first days after meeting Hortense, or re-meeting Hortense after first re-seducing her following their first farewell (how far away it all was!), a Gormanskoï who was fiery, imperious, avid, tireless, insatiable.

The Fake Hortense didn't feel quite herself; he was so like her creator and partner-in-crime, Prince Augre, but with a touch of something extra, i.e., that attraction toward good that evildoers always feel in spite of themselves, a fact revealed to us by treatises on both morals and ethics. She wasn't checked by any moral scruples, deceit was second nature to her, in this case sharpened by her envy and coruscating jealousy of Hortense. In addition, she was acting under orders. She commanded herself to take maximum advantage of the situation.

And this was the downfall; the second downfall, the downfall of this second chapter entitled "The Downfall," the hero's following the heroine's. **In the same way** that Hortense slept unsuspectingly with Prince Acrab'm and not with her lawful lover (and the fact it happened in a bathtub wasn't an attenuating circumstance, not one bit. What's more, although her transgression began in the tub, it continued long afterward in bed), **so likewise** (we *underscore* the parallel relationship, and we *underscore* "underscore") Gormanskoï slept unsuspectingly at the same instant (we won't specify what we specifically mean by "same," because it hinges on a technical definition of the word *slept,* which we can't discuss in this present work) with the Fake Hortense and not with his lawful lover (and the fact it happened on a threadbare carpet in a sordid room in the Bouvard and Pécuchet Hotel in the fine town of Le Havre is not an attenuating circumstance, not in any way, shape or form).

Starting out on the carpet (and he didn't even take the time—no more than Prince Acrab'm did—to get all his clothes off; he was still wearing his socks [red; Acrab'm's were green, which Hortense put out to dry on the balcony later; something the Fake Hortense didn't do with Gormanskoï's because she was a sloppy housekeeper; but why should she have to put the Prince's red socks out to dry? You'll find out when you come to the end of this digression-within-a-digression as well as the main digression itself, and read what follows]) his own transgression, what's more, continued long afterward in the bathtub (full of rust stains from the old pipes). Alas! Six times alas!

But how could Gormanskoï not have had the slightest suspicion that the woman he was holding in his arms, a woman he thought he knew (in the biblical sense—whereas in actual fact he had never laid eyes on her before) wasn't the **real** Hortense? In his defense, we'll say that, given the all-but-perfect resemblance between the Fake Hortense and his own, there was no way he could suspect that this was a case of false advertising. Perhaps due to his aristocratic prejudice as a Poldevian prince, for him the only genuine mutually indiscernible beings were the princes of the Hexarchy; the possibility that Hortense might have an identical "understudy" couldn't even cross his mind. Shouldn't the Fake Hortense's absolutely shameless lovemaking—which did strike him as a bit odd—have given the Prince a clue? No; he thought that she, like himself, was eager because she had been forced to go without. In fact the surprising thing wasn't Hortense's shamelessness; had she ever shown a sense of shame when with him? What a shame that would have been! Hortense always threw herself into her activities enthusiastically and without holding back; all our readers are witness to the fact. What was really and truly odd (and a moment's reflection would have immediately steered him in the right direction) was that Hortense *struck him as shameless;* now that was strange! And what was the cause? Love, of course, who out of affection for his creatures, for the Prince, for the couple (because you can be sure they're going to brave cruel storms), sent Gormanskoï this unconscious message; but he paid it no mind. With a perfectly clear conscience, he fornicated with the Fake Hortense on the carpet, in the bathtub where she led him, in the wardrobe closet (but not in the bed, so dilapidated that it came crashing down after the first few body-thumps).

The fourth part of the novel comes to an end here. Things can't get any worse.

(A reader has observed that we didn't say the Fake Hortense was completely indiscernible from the real one; it's not false [that we haven't, that she isn't]. In order to fool Hortense a prince was needed who really was a perfect outward match with the other [I say perfect match in her eyes with the other; for the trademark she lovingly kissed on the buttock of her presumed lover—I mean of her presumptive partner in love—this mark of the sacred snail, the single feature mutually distinguishing each of the six Princes, and which had allowed her to escape once before from Augre's clutches in the nick of time, looked exactly the way she expected it to look; this fact will be explained in due course, or maybe it won't]. But to fool the Prince, an identical match that wasn't quite so perfect in every detail could do the trick. The Demon Prince didn't create a perfect replica; the Fake Hortense had six flaws, three of which we'll reveal [decency forbids us to mention the others]:
—Firstly, the Fake Hortense had a very slightly pointy navel;
—Secondly, her private tuft spilled over a tiny bit onto her thigh; but most of all,
—Thirdly, a very faint line ran under her left buttock, separating it from her thigh which, as everyone knows, is directly connected to it. However, one of Hortense's most beautiful features was that on her body the two were seamlessly joined. For instance, if you placed your hand on her thigh for a

caress and slid it upward [slipping, for example, under some stray piece of fabric it might by purest accident run across], the moment your hand left her thigh and started caressing her buttock passed unnoticed. One instant you were touching her thigh; the very next, your hand was on her buttock. But despite repeated experiments it always proved impossible to determine at what point you moved from one to the other. It's not hard to imagine the aphrodisiac powers of such uncertainty.)

Part Five

*In Which We Contemplate
Elementary Laws*

Chapter 25

A Heroine's Despair

The afternoon of the next day, January 2nd, just as Hortense and the Prince (whom she still took for another) were reaching the end of an eventful nap in Hortense's bedroom (whose window opened on Avenue de l'Abbé-Migne swarming with pony cabs in front of the entrance gate of Sainte-Gudule Park immediately below and to the right), Prince Augre had his card sent up to request a private audience.

"That fellow's got some nerve," Hortense said.

"Say that you're out," Acrab'm said, nibbling one of her breasts; and he closed her mouth with a kiss, simultaneously muffling his own impulse of remorse by such radical means.

"No, I want you to be here when he comes in and I tell him what I think of his unspeakable conduct."

Prince Augre had a telegram in his pocket sent by the Fake Hortense from Le Havre informing him of the mission's success: "Compromising porno snapshots on the way," and she signed off: "Hugs and kisses." A sardonic smile played over his lips while he waited in the green-papered antechamber before being shown into the suite.

"Madame," he said to Hortense, riveting her with his haughty, arrogant gaze, "I had asked to see you alone; what I have to say is very delicate."

"You can speak in front of my fiancé; I don't keep any secrets from him, you scoundrel!" Hortense said, unable to hold back her anger.

"How beautiful she is, her indignation visibly swelling her breasts under the flimsy fabric she's hastily thrown on," thought both Princes at the same time, one with renewed concupiscence and regret, the other with a memory of recent pleasure and a pang of conscience. "Geez, she's beautiful!" Prince Augre kept his mouth shut, savoring the moment, feeling like Zeus about to cast his lightning bolts against the Titans.

"Well, go on," Hortense said impatiently, "I'm listening; let's get this over with; I can't stand the sight of you, and I wish to end this conversation as quickly as possible; let me repeat: you can talk in front of my fiancé; he won't punish you even though you deserve it."

The Demon Prince scanned the room for a long while, went through the motions of stooping to inspect underneath an armchair, straightened up, and said, with affected nonchalance and feigned surprise: "But I don't see Prince Gormanskoï here, Madame; I see you, the most lovely of all sights, and I see"—at this point he motioned toward Prince Acrab'm with his chin— "I see Prince Acrab'm."

"What," Hortense exclaimed, choking with rage, "giv zyou the right!"

But she stopped short; her glance had just struck Acrab'm and conveyed back—too late, oh far too late—the truth. The funny look which Hortense read on Acrab'm's face in that split second, that combination of shame, resignation, and an already burgeoning nostalgia for that paradise of sensual ecstasy from which he would be barred from now on—forced the sinister truth to dawn upon her instantly. She went pale.

"Madame," Prince Augre said, pretending he had blundered, "I can see that I've spoken thoughtlessly; and I can see that other, cleverer men than myself have been able to beat me to my chosen goal; I remain at your disposal for you know what. Please accept my apologies. But that's not what I had come to inform you about; I'll return when you're alone and your mind's a little clearer."

Then the novel, without laying a finger on him in order to keep its own hands clean, got him out of the room, the palace, and set him down in the street like a Doberman turd. Hortense and Acrab'm remained alone.

"Scoundrel," Hortense said, "how could you have?" And she slapped him back and forth with all her might once, twice, three times, and kept going until she got to six, but she didn't end up feeling any calmer.

"A scoundrel indeed; I have no excuse," he said. "You took me for my brother, I was forbidden to set you right; but later, when I saw you taking your bath, I don't know what happened, I lost my power to resist. I'm ruined now, my life's a mess; I'm a scoundrel."

"I know full well you're a scoundrel," Hortense resumed, slapping him back and forth across the face again, then kicking him in the shins, and stomping on his toes for good measure, etc., etc., a good ten minutes longer.

Stoically the Prince offered his other cheek, other shin, and other foot.

But Hortense's anger gave way to despondency.

"What's going to become of me?" Hortense said. "What am I going to tell him? How will I be able to face seeing him, or him seeing me? Sullied for all time, betrayed, deceived, defiled, and by whom? By his own brother, the man in whom he had the most unshakable trust the world has ever seen. I'm going to go into a convent, I'm going home to mother, I'm going to become my father's assistant in his Haute Cold Cuts business, I'm going to hide myself far from men's eyes with my shame and my despair. I'm going to scrub and scour and scrub myself with a horsehair washcloth, take thirty-seven baths a day; but all the water in the ocean could never wipe clean the stain of moral blood on this sad body of mine," and eloquently she gestured toward her lips, her breasts, her belly.

Prince Acrab'm said nothing; he bowed his head; how beautiful she was, and he, how ashamed!

"But am I not guilty myself? Shouldn't I have been suspicious? How could I have failed to understand that the idiotic poems this happy fool was sending me couldn't have come from the pen of a man so good, so great, so perfect, and so tasteful as my Prince, my lost love, my Gormy?" Hortense continued, following—but too late!—the trail of deductions that we ourselves went down earlier. "But it just occurred to me," she added, her eyes flashing with hatred, looking for the next part of Acrab'm's body she could reduce to pulp, "what about the trademark? You fiddled with the trademark! It was premeditated!"

Acrab'm couldn't let this unfair accusation pass without comment; he had trespassed, certainly, he was a scoundrel, again certainly, but he hadn't done it on purpose, no indeed, it was just one moment of madness ("One moment!" Hortense broke in, "one moment! And since yesterday how many times . . .," with a renewed outbreak of sobbing). Acrab'm then revealed the secret of the trademark, which will be passed on to you in due course—perhaps.

Hortense now heaped all the blame on herself; Acrab'm had nothing to do with it; he was weak, powerless to resist, as simple as that. She knew it was difficult to resist her when she was in certain moods, and even when not. She was the guiltier by far. She started to search her own guilty flesh for something to sternly punish, something to rend, to mar (but within limits), to chastise for its excessive charms (her knees?).

Acrab'm couldn't allow her to call herself guilty. He, he alone, was the scoundrel. He would throw himself at Gormanskoi's feet, he would make a clean breast of everything. He would tell the Prince just how very innocent Hortense was, nothing less than a saint, how he had forced her to do everything she had done, which proved her immense, her pure, her irrepressible love.

"No, no, no," Hortense cried in a paroxysm of guilt. She, a saint? She, pure? Don't make her laugh! Pure? After she   ? A saint, after she. . . ?

The Prince consoled her; he ran a brotherly hand through her hair, around her shoulders; in her distress she huddled against him; her micro-miniskirt rose, her perfume wafted. . . .

They were so close, oh so very close. The Spiral of Sin was lying in wait for them, the terrible downward spiral in which your wrongdoing leads to remorse and repentance that in turn lead to more wrongdoing, over and over until finally you reach your fatal destination, the abyss, or worse: resignation to your weaknesses, or even cynicism. But they exerted the necessary willpower. They got hold of themselves, straightened up, separated, and cast each other wan smiles.

"We've got to take your mind off things, dear Hortense," the Prince said at last. "I'll take you to the Poltengrad Literary Festival."

(Hortense's diary) I'm going to have an awful time getting this happy fool out of my hair!

Chapter 26

The Poltengrad Literary Festival

Located in the Poldevian hinterlands, which are mountainous, Carpathoid, and karstic beyond your wildest dreams, out past the remotest reaches of Lake Melankton in the heart of the Hexarchy, lies the autonomous region of Polentia (capital: Poltengrad). There are three main sources of revenue: corn, goats, and mustaches.

Polenthenians (inhabitants of Polentia) speak a very ancient dialect, a blend of archaic Poldevian and Poldadamian, with a rather substantial Etruscan base; the syntax is part Eskimo, part Basque; the phonetic system, half fish half fowl; in short, a genuine feast for the linguists who descend in droves upon the country.

However, the most remarkable peculiarity of the Polenthenian language, and a great source of concern for its government, is its progressive depletion over the last quarter century: the most commonly used words as well as the most sophisticated vocabulary and syntactic structures aren't simply decaying and on the decline (as everywhere), but actually disappearing at an accelerating pace. And *they are not replaced.* They slip through a hole of oblivion like ozone through the stratosphere. No doubt they're still around in ancient texts and dictionaries; but it's become impossible to use them. Mouths can't pronounce them anymore, typewriters refuse to type them, they vanish from computer monitors, show up as blanks in newspapers. In short, the language is becoming so impoverished that it may well be completely extinct before the sixth centennial celebrations.

The Polenthenian population grew greatly concerned over

this prospect. Such worry might strike us as absurd. In our country an analogous if perhaps somewhat less advanced phenomenon is also occurring, but nobody's worried: how many words on the average does it take to write a newspaper article? A Goncourt Prize-winner? Come up with a number, just to see. But the Polenthenians don't think like us; the disappearance of their words troubles them, all the more so since that's only one of the diagnosed symptoms of their language disease. Some words are invading the semantic territories of others, supplanting them, proliferating, and then disappearing in turn. (To take a recent homegrown example, think of the word *surrealist*, which is now used in any and every situation until it seems like it can mean just about anything.)

Mind you, Polenthenian linguists tell us, this isn't a simple issue of "change." Linguistic change is a completely different matter. In the past, let's say back in the sixth century, you would walk into a café and say: "Give me some *vinem*." All right, years go by, now you walk into a café and say: "Give me some wine." That's the natural form change takes. But nowadays what's happening? You walk into a café and say, "Give me. . . ." " 'Give me' what?" the waiter asks. "Give me. . . ." Nothing comes out. The word *wine* has disappeared from our lips. It's even worse if you're an old Polenthenian with an old-fashioned vocabulary in which the word *wine* still crops up; if you say, "Give me some wine," the waiter won't understand. The word's not a part of his vocabulary anymore. So you wind up saying: "Give me that." "That what?" the waiter says. "This 'that' over here, or that 'that' over there?" So you point with your finger.

The Lagadonians find the whole situation hilarious. These are the inhabitants of the autonomous region of Lagadonia (capital: Lagado), bordering Polentia on the other side of the Faiwmurr Pass (they grant permission to pass through the mountain range separating the two countries for six months a year). What so terrifies the Polenthenians is, on the contrary, the very thing which for Lagadonians signifies that the Polenthenian language is on the right track. For in days of yore (*what's a "yore"?—Reviewer's note*) the Lagadonians themselves abandoned *all* words. They replaced them with things, of which words are never more than the proper names. In Lagadonian there are no words, there are only things themselves, which you carry around with you and present according to the needs of your conversation. Lagadonian is a perfect language, which has been functioning for centuries without complaint. All the same, some pseudomodern minds have recently started to bemoan the obstacles that, according to them, the Lagadonian language has erected on the path of progress: when discussing physics, for example, setting electrons in front of you on the table is extremely awkward, given the well-known quirks of those tiny creatures. Therefore they proposed that the Academy of Lagado hurry completion of its Great Dictionary which is nothing less than an enormous warehouse preserving a replica of every single thing that exists in Lagadonia: each element (therefore thing) of vocabulary is assigned an inventory number serving as a so-called referent to the thing itself, sort of the way money works. But let's forget such nonsense, the old Lagadonians said, and watch and see how the Polenthenians are going to avoid adopting the only effective linguistic reform: our own.

For the time being, the Polenthenians have undertaken a great rescue operation vis-à-vis their language. They decreed a "Lexical Heritage Year"; they offered large bonuses for substantial deposits of sayings, proverbs, and nursery rhymes in the Language Savings Bank; most of all they noticed that imported words weren't as quickly afflicted by the extinction virus. In short, the lexicogenetic heritage, according to some theories, was losing vitality through endogamy, but regenerating itself through exogamy. All travelers to Poldevia are therefore obliged to coin a few phrases when they change money: for instance: "Where there's a will there's a way"; "Pessimistic in judgment, optimistic in will," etc. These foreign phrases are collected and treated in special factories which extract the words and expressions they contain.

Last of all, they came up with the Festival for Literary Internationalism in Polentia, Poldevia, Entelechia, and Ruritania (two associated autonomous regions)—or FLIPPER—to which Acrab'm and Hortense went in order to take their minds off things and not dwell on the difficulties of the days ahead, namely, Gormanskoï's return. The author-applicants from all countries submit copies of their works to the Festival bureau, after which the texts are secretly skinned and sucked to the bone. The awards go to the most lexically rich writings (which doubtlessly explains why, to the general public's surprise, the great novelist Pâquerette d'Azur, who uses at most one hundred or so words in sentences that contain no more than six on the average, has never won the Grand Prize).

There are two prizes: the FLIPPER (the English word *flipper* is the French term for "pinball"—*Translator's note*) for a novel, and the FLIPPER for poetry. The aim of the poetry prize was to enrich family and rural vocabulary: this is why only two genres of contemporary poetry are encouraged:

—verse of the "I've two big oxen in my stable / Two big white oxen spotted red" genre;

—or verse of the "There was a wardrobe dimly polished / That heard the voice of my great aunts" genre (which is in all probability the reason why these same two genres are presently flourishing in our country).

Another condition was for each poem to contain enough words to make their linguistic exploitation economically viable: vehemently excluded were those incredible works having virtually blank pages with almost nothing printed on them.

The Grand FLIPPER Prizes were gold snails worth a fortune. After the jury's decisions were announced the snails were solemnly presented to the prizewinners by a celebrity. That year, once word got around she was in Polentia, Hortense

151

was the unanimous choice as the presenter. The prizewinner accepted the trophy from her beautiful hands. He was a tall, bald man with an intelligent, distinguished face, profoundly weathered by a stormy century; he was wearing a ripped pullover, a greenish Burberry raincoat, worn corduroy trousers and espadrilles: a green one on his right foot, a red on his left. In one hand he held a copy of the day's *Times;* in the other, a yellow bag marked with "Big Shopper" (in English) from the top of which jutted a leek.

The award ceremony was presided over by the alcalde (the name of the official formerly going by the name of "mayor," a word which had been lost; the new title had been excerpted from last year's prizewinning novel) with the entire council present. All the council members, including the alcalde, and the near-totality of adults in Polentia, had mustaches and were, therefore, bandits. This is why, once the ceremony ended, they hid in ambush at the city outskirts and attacked the six-pony stagecoach carrying the prizewinners. They swiped the gold snails and went home. The gold snails never left Polentia; likewise, the language didn't lose the word *snail.*

Meanwhile, the local paper announced that Gormanskoı was due back in Queneau'stown: he was said to be accompanied by his fiancée, the beautiful Miss Hortense. "What!" Hortense and Acrab'm exclaimed in unison. They hurried their way home.

Chapter 27

Such a Beautiful Word: Jealousy

The language disease infecting the province of Polentia is also present in an endemic, although far less serious form throughout Poldevia. There, too, some words have vanished, often leading to the concurrent disappearance of what they were both duty- and honor-bound to designate. Such disappearances can affect the whole population, or only certain segments. In particular the six compossible worlds coexisting in these beautiful regions are affected in different ways. The Poldadamists are unfamiliar with certain words frequented by the Poldevians; and vice versa. The same inequality marks individuals: some people don't know certain words; others don't know any. For some people the word *tomato* evokes a red object; for others, a green, orange, or blue (?) one; and they're all correct, each according to his or her own personal free-for-all worldview. Aren't tomatoes green when you pickle them? Red, when you throw them at a soprano? For others still the word *tomato* means nothing; you say "tomato" and no object pops up in front of their inner eye; the word's absence has forced the thing to disappear. You show them a tomato and they don't see anything.

As their reunion with Gormanskoï approached, Hortense and Acrab'm anguished over their shameful yet necessary confession; but they also had a question or two: just who was this "Hortense" the Presumed Premier Prince had picked up in Le Havre? An imposter no doubt, but an imposter capable of fooling the Prince? Was such a thing even imaginable? They were a step away from guessing the truth; their final clue would be figuring out the malicious cause behind such an occurrence.

Meanwhile, her mission accomplished, the Fake Hortense had rejoined her lord and master in his picture chamber, and in his arms was fine-tuning her knowledge of the erotic contrasts between good and evil. The result was that only a single Hortense at any one time was available on the market. And so Gormanskoï, seeing her in Acrab'm's company, didn't suspect for a moment that now there were two of them.

And how could he be set straight? They didn't dare risk it. Gormanskoï told them with a laugh that he wasn't sorry about his orders being disobeyed since he had gotten so very much out of it. They didn't understand what he was referring to; they were pained and completely preoccupied by their sin and confession. Gormanskoï lent them his kind, bemused attention; he wanted to know exactly when, and what. **He wasn't jealous.** He didn't know what jealousy was; he had never heard the word, nor felt the emotion.

"What's this?" Hortense said in the end, relieved but at the same time offended, "you're not jealous?"

"Huh?" he said, "what did you say?"

Hortense repeated: "You don't feel any jealousy at the idea that I, that we . . ."

"Feel what? Poldevian verbs, my dear Hortense, love their complements. If you say, 'You don't feel . . . at the idea that, period,' your sentence structure's wrong. We say: 'You don't feel x at the idea of y,' in which x stands for a noun, any noun at all, tomato for instance: 'You don't feel any tomato at the idea that I slept y-number of times in two days with Acrab'm?' Such is the inexorable syntactic law of the Poldevian language; if you don't respect it, a native speaker can't understand your sentence."

Thus spoke Gormanskoï, with the kindness of a lover and a prince. He gave great attention to Hortense's progress in mastering Poldevian; the future wife of a soon-to-be Reigning Prince is duty-bound to possess perfect command of the language. Hortense saw that he had missed something. So she repeated herself, pronouncing slowly and distinctly, in a 14-point bold embossed Monaco font, the Poldevian word for *jealousy:* "Don't you feel any **JEALOUSY** at the idea that I slept so passionately and so many times with Acrab'm?"

This time the word reached Gormanskoï's ears. For the first time he heard the word *jealousy.* He repeated it with interest, surprise, wariness. He found it beautiful: *"Jealousy, jealousy,* what a beautiful word," he said. "I thought I'd completely forgotten it [a well-known psychological phenomenon called "déjà-vu syndrome"]. I'd rate it halfway between *sock* and *fanlight,* slightly more pungent than *mucilage;* not bad at all [this comment can't be understood by those without an in-depth command of Poldevian phonology and etymology, impossible to expand upon within the limited scope of the present work which is, may we remind our reviewers once again, a novel and not a treatise on linguistics]. What does it mean?"

He had caught the word, but its meaning eluded him.

Hortense thought he was joking. Once again this proved he wasn't jealous and that, consequently, she hadn't done anything wrong, at least in his eyes. It was surprising, although when you came down to it, typically Poldevian.

But in fact he wasn't joking at all; Hortense's stubborn insistence had just forced the word *jealousy* into his vocabulary.

Meanwhile, since Gormanskoï was presently expected by the Reigning Prince in order to convey the compliments of the city of Le Havre, he took leave of them. Prince Acrab'm and Hortense found themselves alone again. For one brief second Hortense was tempted. Since Gormanskoï greeted this terrible mix-up good-naturedly, almost indifferently, why lose any sleep over it? Admittedly, Acrab'm wasn't her fiancé; he was a bit of a nitwit (a big nitwit in fact), a little shy, bursting with energy although at times a little awkward. But while waiting for the Prince to start showing her the old receptive self she was used to, couldn't she? And she could see with her own eyes that Acrab'm had the same idea. With a truly princelike swiftness and nonchalance he adapted to the new situation and was already starting to take her clothes off.

She went on: if Gormanskoï wasn't jealous, she had a duty to be jealous for both of them; she had to be worthy of her love, and faithful, as she always would have remained if she hadn't been led astray by circumstances. So she buttoned back up the six buttons already unbuttoned by Acrab'm along her thigh and said: "Friends?"

"Friends," he answered without insisting.

From now on he would love her from afar, chastely, like a sister, keeping in the secret garden of his memory those precious, incredible hours, now gone forever, when he had—yes, when he had. . . .

Alcius, the Reigning Prince, was furious: not only had those two dimwitted secret agents, Misters T. and T., proved incapable of rendering Prince Airt'n harmless (by getting the Le Havre police to arrest him for disturbing the peace, resisting arrest, and assault and battery against traffic cops; given all the legal tricks at their disposal, this would have kept the Prince away from Poldevia for at least a month, just the time Alcius needed to reach a real power-sharing agreement with Augre). But what's more, once back in Queneau'stown, they went on a nonstop drinking binge under the pretext of holiday get-togethers with their families.

The date was Wednesday, January 3rd: the Prince was furious in his office where Misters T. and T., badly hung over, were simultaneously shuffling their feet in embarrassment and wringing their professional "wall-colored" raincoats in their jittery hands. He gave another glance at the report from secret agent John LeCircle, whom he had sent to Le Havre to keep an eye on the work of his two secret agents Misters T. and T.

"I'm talking to you, Tweedledum!" Alcius inveighed (he had just found the word *inveighed* in his morning paper). "Answer me: how could you have let him escape and come back here?"

Misters T. and T. stood speechless.

"Is that you, Tweedledum?" he said to the one on his left.

"I'm Tweedledum," answered the other.

"If that's true," the first one said, "then I'm Tweedledee."

Alcius tore a page from the scratch pad on his desk and, taking into account Misters T. and T.'s characteristics, set about tackling the problem posed by these two statements; but he didn't come up with any solution.

"Get the hell out of here," he said at last, exasperated.

Misters T. and T. left.

"You know, Mr. T.," Tweedledum said to Tweedledee after they sat down at the Pony Shoe in front of two extra-strength double Poldevian espressos (here a double Poldevian espresso goes by the name of "Mathews," i.e., a double serving in a single demitasse, since the product must remain constant and equal to one unit), "I basically think he's stupid."

"You're wrong," Mr. T. answered Tweedledee in approval.

Chapter 28

Laurie and Carlotta Leave for Poldevia

It's masks-off time. The Author's here! He's the man you've been crossing paths with all through these pages. Back in Chapter 5 for instance, do you remember: "They crossed paths with a tall, bald, distinguished man beaming with intelligence, whose face had been weathered by a stormy century; he was wearing a ripped pullover, a greenish Burberry raincoat, worn corduroy trousers, and espadrilles—a blue one on his left foot, a black on his right; in one hand he held a copy of the day's *Times;* in the other, a red bag marked with 'Big Shopper' (in English) from the top of which jutted a leek." That's him, always hard at work, pouring all his energy into the story to keep it running smoothly, while remaining anonymous himself, virtually underground.

And what explains this? Publisher's orders! A month ago the Publisher had me in his office to sign my contract; after glancing at the file his secretary put together in order to reacquaint him with my name (along with the sales performance of my preceding work; as I bent over the desk while pretending to look for an ashtray [I don't smoke], I managed to read the following bits of information: the week of —— to the —— [this was the first month after publication] orders filled: 6; returns: 317; what does that mean?), he said to me: "And we'll set the delivery deadline for the mackintoshuscript thirty-seven days after the present contract is signed—is that all right with you?" I answered that it was; the deadline seemed reasonable (I was planning thirty-seven chapters).

I was about to take my leave when I noticed there was something else; he looked unresolved about something, answering then hanging up his four telephone receivers one after the other; at last he made up his mind to speak: "My dear Roubaud, you know I don't have any advice to give you about writing; you're the author, you write whatever pops into your head; you hand it over to me and then it's up to me to take all the risks; I know, it's all part of the profession. Which is why you'll understand that I didn't resolve to tell you what I am about to say without very serious reasons.

"My dear Roubaud, you're much too visible in your novels. I know full well that all novels are autobiographical, but come on now, really, a writer *transposes*, he *transposes*. By contrast you're there all the time, you intervene, have discussions with your characters, or the reader, you explain what you've done, what you're doing, what you're going to do, here's the author, there's the author—how do you expect the reading public to learn their way around!"

In short he laid down his conditions: I was to put off my appearance until the latest possible moment, at any rate some place after the first chapter in order to make it reasonably certain that no reviewers would chance upon it. I had to bow to his demand.

The Publisher sighed as he watched the Author go off; then he moved on to serious things: his all-but-sealed contract with J. A. for a sociosemiological interpretation of that Moment's fundamental two-part question:

"Should a simplified spelling system be taught to young girls who wear chadars?" (If J. A. proved too greedy, he always had E. M. as a standby.)

I kept my promise; it's only today, in Chapter 28, that at last I'm speaking in my name, the Author. Of course, this necessarily entailed major difficulties when constructing the work. Let one example suffice: you certainly had a hard time believing that Ophelia so easily agreed to leave her life of comfort in the apartment of her two loving foster parents, Carlotta and Laurie, so she could go and act as Hortense's understudy in a battle whose outcome was uncertain, under the sole protection of Jim Wedderburn, and despite Laurie and Carlotta's lack of enthusiasm for the plan. And indeed it was I, the Author, who got her to agree to everything in the course of a private chat she very gladly granted me but which I was unable to recount at the proper time. An excellent photograph of our conversation taken by Laure Durien exists, but for stingy cost-cutting reasons the French publisher wouldn't allow it to be reproduced at this point in the book. Nor did he even consent for it to be substituted by a brief statement I wrote which ran more or less as follows:

Due to the uncooperativeness of a certain segment of our staff it was not possible to reproduce here the photograph of the meeting between the Author and Ophelia; we extend our apologies.

The printer.

(The American publisher, by contrast, magnanimously agreed to reproduce the photo here, per the Author's original wish—*Translator's note.*)

I accompanied Laurie and Carlotta to the Marché des Bébés Oranges. They had very kindly invited me to lunch; we bought some Poldevian mountain ham at the butcher's (a native of those regions), one of Carlotta's young male admirers. He was very proud of his new automated register, which also did additions as he had just discovered.

We sat in the kitchen; Laurie prepared the lunch; the Author and Carlotta put their feet under the table. Carlotta, a subscriber to *For Poldevian Science,* a sophisticated scientific journal, our country's edition of the famous *Scientific Poldevian,* was immersed in the most recent issue. One article in particular drew her attention.

"Did you know," she said, "that eggs feel pain? It's just been irrefutably proven by the following experiment carried out by a team of psychologists from the University of Queneau'stown. You take three eggs, place them on a table in front of which a student is seated. Into each egg unobtrusive and ultrasensitive electrodes have been introduced, and the egg's brain waves appear on a monitor. At the start of the experiment all the waves are normal. At a signal the student picks up an egg and swallows it whole. The monitor of this egg shows a flat encephalogram. And at the same instant on the screens representing the mental states of the second and third eggs there appear signs of frenzied agitation, waves of panicky terror. The student picks up the second egg and swallows it whole. And on the third egg's screen: a blank. It fainted!"

"Do you want eggs for starters?" Laurie asked.

Later, while we were finishing up the salmon steak—which Laurie washed down with some Saint-Joseph's white and the Author with root beer (marvelous "beer from roots" made from a flavored burnt-tire base, my favorite beverage, but hard to find in our country, which Laurie and Carlotta dig up in a supermarket on Rue des Citoyens and serve me when I visit; such kind thoughtfulness— *Author's note*); and Carlotta with orange juice.

"How happy Ophelia would have been!" Carlotta said.

"When's she getting back?"

"Well now," I began with some embarrassment, for I absolutely had to speak out in my defense; I needed, absolutely needed all three of them to be present in Poldevia for at least the last part of the book where serious storm clouds were building; their initial refusal to travel there—which caught me by total surprise—created enormous structural problems for my novel; but now it was far worse, I was flirting with disaster.

The doorbell rang. Laurie went to open up: "Hotello!" she said. It was he. Hotello had been the two redheads' cat before Ophelia. During the events narrated in one of the Author's preceding novels, he had helped them foil—with the participation of the pony Cyrandzoï—the Demon Prince's anti-Hortensian schemes; then, once his job was done, he had disappeared; he had gone back to Poldevia, his homeland. For Hotello was none other than Alexandre Vladimirovitch (the father, we discovered the same time as she did, of Ophelia). Prince Gormanskoï had sent him here to add his plea for Laurie and Carlotta's help.

While on this subject, let me point out a curious fact: when in my third and present book I set about telling what happened, I went to my Publisher's office to sign the contract. But precisely on this very day, when Laurie got home, she found Hotello on her doormat after an eighteen-month-long absence without a word: "Well, I'll be," Laurie said, "what are you doing here?"

Without answering Hotello entered with her, walked into the kitchen, ate from Ophelia's dish, went over and made himself comfortable in her favorite armchair (Ophelia was a bit taken aback), then left as he had come. The explanation for this strange coincidence is very simple and as follows: when Gormanskoï suggested to Alexandre Vladimirovitch that he come to our country and request Laurie and Carlotta's help, he left immediately (eventually arriving at the moment we've indicated); but at the outset he had absentmindedly triggered a "space-time warping of the chronoclastic infindibulum" (cats, who far surpass us in their ability to travel through the continuum, do lose their way sometimes) and he made his first appearance on Laurie's doorstep *more than eighteen months before the date of the planned visit.* So he had to start all over again. That clears that up.

Alexandre Vladimirovitch-Hotello chimed in with me to persuade them. Laurie and Carlotta consulted their respective dance cards and finally said: "We can't leave Hortense and Ophelia in such dire straits."

and

"All right, but, as we've already said, no more than one weekend."

I had to make do with that. (In reality they stayed nine days.)

Chapter 29

The Importance of Being Faithful, or Girltalk

On the night table in Hortense's bedroom was a heavily annotated critical edition of Spinoza's *Ethics*. At the foot of the bed, strewn over the floor, were drafts of letters, a pile of books: *Die Entfuhrung des Gertrude Stein* (a German translation of a novel by Pâquerette d'Azur); several works in the "Charles and Queen" collection: classics like *Virgin and Mother; Virgin and Floozy . . .* and modern titles: *Sensual Stew, I'm Not Batavia, The Serfs of Love, The Female Stranger of Monteverdi* (the sequel to *The Female Stranger Whose Cat Mews*).

At first, Hortense was reluctant to speak. She wanted their advice. About what? Hortense didn't want to "tell everything," she was ashamed. She was looking for some general advice on a universal problem. Laurie and Carlotta gave each other a glance. Ophelia, so situated on Hortense's lap that she could lovingly gaze upon Laurie and Carlotta by turns, looked up at her (observation: Chapter 29 is located, chronologically, after the present chapter; please refer to what follows).

"Tell us anyway."

Hortense: "I'd like to know what you think about fidelity."

Laurie: "Whose?"

Carlotta: "We're not the Fidelity Hotline."

Laurie: "Do you think we should start up a 900 number for Hortense, the messenger of fidelity? A 1-800 number's cheaper."

Hortense: "Seriously, please, this is vital."

Carlotta: "She wants to be unfaithful."

Laurie: "She what?"

Hortense: "What 'what'?"

Laurie: "Who?"

Hortense (upset): "That's not it at all: it's a theoretical problem of the utmost importance for my happiness and the way I look at life."

Laurie, Carlotta, Ophelia: "All right, all right, all right, OK, OK, OK, we don't want to know."

Laurie: "First of all, what do you mean by 'faithful'?"

Hortense: "Fidelity is plain and simply, as you know full well, a constancy in your affections, your feelings; a person is faithful when she (or he) has sexual relations only with him (or her) to whom she (or he) is sworn."

Ophelia: "Why all these parenthetical interjections? I'm completely faithful to Carlotta and Laurie; and I'm a she, and they're shes."

Laurie: "First of all, you're confusing constancy with fidelity. Do you love your Prince?"

Hortense: "I love him, he's the Prince of my life and I'm crazy about him."

Laurie: "As a result you love him with constancy, since constancy is the quality of that which never stops being the same. You are constant and 'faithful,' according to the first meaning of the word. But in what way does that force you to be faithful in the second sense, which has a slightly different nuance. The second sense means 'being faithful to one's post.' "

Ophelia: " 'Post'? Who's that?"

Carlotta: "Ophelia, mind your own business!"

Laurie: "Ophelia, don't keep interrupting all the time with idiotic questions."

Ophelia (offended): "Fine, I just. . . ."

Hortense: "But can I stay the same while loving another?"

Carlotta: "How can you stop being the same as yourself? Be logical."

Hortense: "But how can I be constant while changing in love?"

Laurie: "Who's saying anything about 'changing in love'? The definition of constancy in no way implies unicity."

Carlotta: "Love isn't the **Parmedian One**."

Then Carlotta cruelly reminded her that, in one of her previous adventures, she had been married and it wasn't to the Prince. But Hortense answered that she had never loved her husband, and it was only from the moment she met the Prince, in one absolute and blessed second, at the Flaubert Hotel in Bacon-les-Mouilleres, that the eternity of her love had begun.

Carlotta: "Can eternity have a beginning?"

Laurie: "Please, let's not get off the subject. *(To Hortense:)* But when you fornicated with the Prince in the Flaubert Hotel, weren't you being unfaithful to your husband? Weren't you disloyal, perfidious, rebellious, treacherous, adulterous, inconstant, and fickle? Not to mention perjurious and unpunctual?"

Hortense: "Yes, but I didn't love the other man."

Laurie: "So does it mean that since you love you must forbid yourself from looking elsewhere? From playing in the big kids' playground when the chance comes up? From being 'unfaithful' in the second sense, part b?"

Hortense: "That's what I'm asking you: what have you got to say?"

Laurie and Carlotta: "We're telling you to do as you like."

Hortense: "But then, what if he. . . ?"

Laurie and Carlotta: "He must be faithful in the first and second sense, plus the second sense part b. And you can let your eyes wander and drive all the wild guys wild."

Carlotta: "What we've just said presents one problem—because you can drive only those guys wild who are alone, since if they're not alone, the reason is there's a special woman who loves them and whom they love, and by virtue of our reasoning they are duty-bound to show her constancy and fidelity in the first, second, and second sense part b, plus all the others we haven't mentioned."

Ophelia: "You're just saying that because you're a Kantian."

Laurie: "It's good enough to be a Kantian locally, if that's what's bothering you. You can look around, but at a distance."

Hortense (interested): "Then don't you think the situation's not symmetrical? We're free, except locally, and he isn't?"

Laurie and Carlotta: "It's very simple; everybody does what they want. We do as we want; and they do as they want. But stop and think for a minute. What can this Prince of yours want? To be in love with you, just you, and nobody else, forever."

Hortense: "Like I want?"

Laurie and Carlotta: "What's this 'like you want'? Like he wants, like he has no choice but to want any other way since he loves you. So there we have it. Now you're going to tell us what's really going on, we'll give you our opinion, but strictly between ourselves, it's none of the Reader's business."

(This passage has eluded the Author, who would have certainly suppressed it if he had seen it.)

"It's none of the Author's business either," Hortense said, carefully closing the bedroom door, then giving it a quick flip open to check and see whether anybody had his ear pressed against it. "I agree with you. I'd like you to help me get out of here—along with the Prince, if he drops the idea he's Hamlet; but—and I won't mince my words—if necessary, without him. It's true that I love him, I can't help myself, but I can't help myself from doing a little thinking either, contrary to what some people think."

This was quite a mouthful to be coming out of Hortense; Laurie and Carlotta weren't used to it.

"Should have given us a hint," they said, "we wouldn't have called you a bimbo . . . or an airhead," Carlotta added.

"You called me an airhead?"

"No, but it was on the tip of my tongue."

"I've got some bimbo in me, sometimes," Hortense said, "I know; maybe I've studied too much philosophy, that's possible; unless it's because of my knees."

167

"What's the matter with your knees?" Carlotta asked.

"Let's not get off the subject," Laurie said.

"I've got some bimbo in me, maybe," Hortense said, "but not as much as that. It's the Author and the Poldevians who are bimbofying me; that's how they see me and they're the ones telling the story; but I fully intend to react; if necessary, I'll pay the Publisher a visit."

"We'll tell him ourselves," Laurie and Carlotta said.

"Do you think he still loves me?" Hortense asked pensively.

"Are you going to start that all over again?" said Carlotta.

"No," Hortense said, "not Gormanskoï; the Author."

The two redheads swore to her that the feelings the Author had for her hadn't changed. They knew through Jim Wedderburn and Ophelia.

"Fine. Now you're going to explain to us what's *really* going on."

Chapter 30

Men, Books, and Redheads

I had accompanied Hortense to the Queneau'stown airport to welcome Laurie and Carlotta. We took a pony cart back to Hortense's place; by "we," I mean the Author, Hortense herself, and Laurie—Carlotta went on ahead, galloping with Cyrandzoï, an old friend from previous adventures. I say "Hortense's place," because the apartment she occupied in her fiancé the Prince's palace, while still belonging to the Prince in name, had become for all practical purposes her own. The Prince, for dynastic and strategic reasons, continued to reside at his mother's.

Mother and daughter gave the premises the once-over with a critical eye. They picked out their rooms: a bedroom with a mezzanine for Carlotta; and one with a balcony and view over Sainte-Gudule Cathedral and park for Laurie. They tried out the bathroom, which met with their approval. The dominant red color scheme made them wince, but didn't surprise them; Poldevian taste is so Poldevian! Laurie added a few nominal(ist) touches to allow for smoother and more efficient operations: on the ceilings she wrote in a legible hand: "ceiling"; "hot water" above the hot water faucets, etc. She pinned up a map of the neighborhood on their kitchen wall, marking the correct spot with "You Are Here." Along with the map, an arrow aimed in the general geographic direction of the City clearly pointed: "Homeward."

Once this was done, she took a shower, borrowed one of Hortense's bathrobes, called Carlotta up from the park where she was prancing about with Cyrandzoï, had that serious conversation with Hortense about the problems of Love and Fidelity that we have, in a flash-forward (for architectural reasons that have no interest for the reader) reported in the previous chapter, Chapter 29.

But let there be no misunderstanding. We absolutely are not making any petty insistence that the Reader (male or female) be shut out. On the contrary, we've thrown these pages wide open toward him (or her), we've invited the Reader into Hortense's tub, we've explained everything, absolutely every single thing needed to understand the novel. We hold only one advantage: we're out in front. And the Reader can never catch up. This statement is easy to prove. In order to catch up to us the Reader must get to the end of what we're writing; but when he reaches the end of what we've written, at this very moment for instance, we're already further along. And to get to where we are now he must necessarily pass the point we've already been. **He'll always lag behind.** It's irrefutable. This element of superiority is enough for us; we don't need to add omniscience, omission, or dissimulation.

I paid a visit to the travelers on the next and succeeding days. They bitched and moaned. "Can you believe this climate?" It was raining. I asked them if they had done any sight-seeing. They had gone to the Leeiff Tower, the jewel of Poldevian Gothic art, shaped like an X and 2 x 317 meters high (a world record, the envy of France, New York, Chicago, and the Japanese); they came back soaked to the bone. Since then, they had been staying in bed, listening to compact discs, or reading; Laurie drank tea, Carlotta made crepes, which she shared with Cyrandzoï, who slept on the living room carpet.

"Basically," they told me, "it's just like being home, only bigger."

"Yes," Carlotta added, "geometrically speaking, we set up a ratio six similarity with a very slight rotation vis-à-vis the sun, and we got it just right."

I admitted that there was indeed a certain resemblance, but

added foolishly that since this was the case, they shouldn't feel homesick.

"So then what good's Poldevia if it's just like home?"

I was amazed by such unfairness.

"Don't whine," Carlotta said, "he's going to start whining again, like when we go out and he comes over for Ophelia to console him; by the way, when's she coming back?"

It was vital that I proceed with the most elementary caution. Ophelia rang the doorbell.

She headed straight for Carlotta, leaped into her arms; they rubbed muzzles and nibbled at each other as always after having been apart. Then Ophelia went over to say hello to Laurie on her bed. "Poor Ophelia!" Laurie said, "poor, poor Ophelia!" ("Poor, poor Ophelia" is uttered solemnly, with conviction and pity, heavily stressing the first syllable and then along a descending rhythm à la Monteverdi, ending on an exclamation point [slightly tinged with irony]; repeat after me: "**Poor,** poor Ophelia!") Ophelia actually did feel she was an object of pity, and pitiful. She stretched her muzzle toward Laurie and squeaked out a meow, pitifully. Then she called for *kasscroot'*.

Ophelia, who had been reunited with her parents in Chapter 21 (don't tell me you've forgotten already), had accompanied Tioutcha, her redfurred mother, to her small, modest suburban bungalow, and rediscovered with emotion her old childhood haunts: pushing open the narrow, rickety door, she strolled through the small garden; the fountain still made its silvery purl, and the old gardener still quavered out his undying complaint ("Don't play with my roses, Missy Ophelia!"); she even found Velleda still standing, the German prophetess of the first century who led the revolt of the Batavians against the Roman yoke and whom people made statues of; her plaster was flaking away at the end of the lane amid the faded fragrance of reseda ("Where there're roses there's reseda," as the song goes). Once again she saw the pomegranate tree where she had chased her first field mouse; the section of peeling wall where her first lizard had disappeared, leaving behind its tail. But duty recalled her to Queneau'stown. "Good-bye, Mommy, meow." "Meow, dear daughter, at least pick up the phone once in a while!"

I took advantage of Ophelia's homecoming (she came over to sharpen her claws on my trousers and nestle on my lap in a position that allowed her to cast long, loving looks toward Carlotta or Laurie) to expose my architectural problems. If it's true, as literary theoreticians have amply demonstrated, that a Man is his Work, and vice versa, we should also bear in mind that the transition between them must be *mediated;* by that I don't mean broadcast on television (which can help the novel's sales, but not necessarily its composition); I mean that some element outside the two terms interlinked by the Principle of Identity $M = W$ (or, if there are two works of literature, $M = tWo$) must play a mediating role in order to establish both their essential equality and their metaphoric distance, if I may be so bold as to express myself in such language.

To accomplish this, a redheaded woman is an absolute must; and all the better with two. I very quickly caught on to this point, which gives me an undeniable advantage over my fellow novelists (noticed very early on by a reviewer with uncommon intuition in the *Independent of the Southern Coast and the Northern Minervois Region,* reprinted several times, notably in the *Memphis Scimitar* in Tennessee).

Admittedly (I wonder what that "admittedly" is doing here— *Author's note;* but since it's there I'll let it be) it's not so much that a redheaded woman, either over the phone or live and in person, is able to provide you with technical advice, or any of those various assessments, informative tidbits, or expressions furnishing the bedrock and piquancy of all narratives, and which you then need only to transcribe word for word in the chapter you are making appear (guided by the divine blaze of inspiration) on your computer screen. Instead, the special contribution of redheads is their ability to act as seismographs in human affairs. As quickly as cats (explaining their somewhat identical

172

outlooks) they record the emotional currents, the personality vibrations, the genuine motives behind human (or penguin) actions concealed by speech; in short, everything a novelist finds an absolute must for his task of deciphering some meaning in the incomprehensible, entangled web of nerve-wracking events. I've thought long and hard about these questions, explaining the profundity that imbues what I've just written.

So here I insist on publicly acknowledging all that my novel owes to Laurie and Carlotta; at least (if I can judge by their screwed-up faces) all that I *understood* in my own personal way, based on their reports and interpretation of events.

This was the very day I informed them of my difficulties with Chapter 29, which they gladly made up their minds to help me resolve.

(A related question: on this occasion I had noticed that Hortense, before speaking to Laurie and Carlotta, in order to get some sense of her moral dilemma, had sought inspiration in Spinoza, but also in a certain number of novels from the collection—very popular in Poldevia—called "Charles and Queen" [it's in this collection that a translation of Pâquerette d'Azur's famous novel, *The Lover,* has just appeared]. Wouldn't she have been better inspired by reading the works of M. P., who is praised to the skies? "Not at all," Laurie said, "the novels in the Charles and Queen collection are totally worthless and idiotic; but that's just the point, everybody *knows* they're worthless and idiotic, so they allow you to draw unquestionable conclusions. With any other novel, on the contrary, you don't know before reading it [if you've made the right and proper decision, just as the first Poldevian philosopher, Parmenidzoï, long ago advised, namely, to follow the Path of Truth and not the ever-so-fallible Path of Opinion] whether or not it's worthless or idiotic; and more often than not you don't know until finishing it [and even then . . .]. But it's too late to draw any lesson whatsoever." Which is why, like Carlotta, Hortense read "Charles and Queen" books, and she was right to do so.)

Part Six

*The Classic Tearful Parting
from the Attractions of
a Novel Nearing Its End*

Chapter 31

O How Very Unhappy the Othello Whose Iago Is Desdemona!

Prince Augre and the Fake Hortense (or the "Wrong" Hortense, whom, for simplicity's sake, we'll refer to as WHortense for the remainder of the story) having mutually congratulated each other over the smooth success of their scheme in the way you can imagine (I leave you the responsibility for your own fantasies), joined forces again to plot the next steps. The negotiations with the Prince had gone nowhere; the Reigning Prince was probably thinking that he'd get out of his jam all by himself with the help of his "pseudo-Hamlet" (an intrigue from another age); clearly he underestimated Gormanskoï, and most of all Alexandre Vladimirovitch. Augre's spies informed him about Laurie and Carlotta's arrival; like all Demon Princes he harbored a genuine fear and hatred of redheaded women; for the first time he had misgivings. But it would take far more than that for him to give up. Surrendering wasn't in his nature. So he needed to push onward with Operation #2, which had already been set into motion.

The second operation was modeled after another play in the great Poldevian theatrical repertoire (also copied by Shahkayspear): *Othello*. **Suspicion** had to be planted in Gormanskoï's soul so that he would be consumed with **jealousy,** and brought to identify himself with Othello; Hortense would be cast in the role of Desdemona (her name was Testimony in the authentic version; "Desdemona" is most probably a translation error). Then it would all go off like clockwork: Gormanskoï-Othello would smother Hortense-Desdemona under pillows ordered from the *Corte Poldevez, el gran magazin,* on Place Queneleieff. Or, more likely, since capital crimes and capital punishment have been virtually unknown in Poldevia since the age of Prince Arnaut Danieldzoï, he'd throw Desdemona down on top of the pillows, lift her skirt, lower her panties, and administer a sound spanking before he sent her packing. In either case he'd wind up without a fiancée, so he could no longer aspire to be Reigning Prince; Alcius would remain in power (but forced into an alliance with Augre, for the latter would keep a video recording of the whole deal which he could use to pressure the old crook if he sensed Alcius had even the slightest inclination to pull any funny stuff).

The special villainy of the Machiavellian plan rests on one particular feature of the oldest-known version of *Othello,* the *Ur-Othello* of sorts, namely, the sixth story of the sixth part of the *Hecatommithi* by Giraldi Cinthio, published in Venice in 1565, and dropped for reasons unknown by Shahkayspear. Nevertheless, it is given a masterful treatment in the Poldevian *Othello* from which Augre took his inspiration. It can be summarized in one sentence: **"O how very unhappy the Othello whose Iago is Desdemona."**

Now isn't that the truth.

"Here's what we're going to do," he said into the ear of WHortense (we should remind you that since the start of this chapter and throughout the rest of the story, this abbreviated name designates Augre's accomplice, the erroneous and deceitful lover of Gormanskoï, the Fake or Wrong Hortense).

The clairvoyance of cats appears in all its glory during the course of this next episode. Indeed, what was the pseudonym chosen by Alexandre Vladimirovitch during his incognito trip to our City for the purpose of foiling the traps set (way back then, already) by the very same Prince Augre (who in those days was going by his other name, K'manoroïgs), on learning there was a new opening for a cat at Laurie and Carlotta's after

Liilii's pussynapping (the smartest cat of her generation; to this day no one has claimed responsibility for this abduction which remains unexplained), and he needed a cover identity before showing up and getting hired on the spot? Hotello! (Hotello is the pseudonym for Alexandre Vladimirovitch announced at the start of the preceding sentence—*Note for the benefit of my reviewers*). Now if you take this name Hotello and move the first H two places to the right, what do you get? Othello! But Prince Augre's plans for the future (a future perfect, not yet realized, therefore susceptible to changes) were based not on the story of a man of color from Venezia, but on another by Carmen Debizet. And so Hotello had first gone by the name of Carmen; but the veterinarian where Carlotta brought him (her) for something called a "whiskers cold," blew to pieces his original cover by exclaiming: "*He*'s such a handsome cat!" Al. Vl. had to make like he had been misunderstood, that "Carmen Debizet" was his mother's name and that, in fact, his own was Hotello. This simultaneously triggered, more than two years ahead of schedule (how time flies! Carlotta's going to turn eighteen! Everything flitters, fritters, and fizzles away all too quickly, as Saint Augustine says; very soon perhaps a sign will appear on her door one fine morning just like on my niece Marianne's in the past—"Do not disturb, I'm over twenty-one!"),

this simultaneously threw off, more than two years ahead of schedule, the already very detailed plans (two years into the future is quite something!) of Prince Augre, and considerably improved the quality of the intrigue whose scenario, in the first version of the future, was rather rickety. Where is the author who will fulfill the crying need for the book *The Role of Great Cats Throughout History?*

For, in the Poldevian *Othello,* through impudent, wily, and childish perversity that perfectly befits what is at bottom our author-genius's rather misogynist conception, after losing the handkerchief (Desdemona's, not the playwright's), and not wanting to confess the fact to her husband as a way of punishing him for reproaching her, Desdemona is the one who prefers to leak drop by drop into his previously suspicion-proof soul (like Gormanskoï, he has never heard the word, the same for jealousy, and hence the faintest glimmer of suspicion or jealousy can't cross his mind) the acidlike possibility of her own infidelity. The play shows us how she happens to read—it's explicitly stated in the stage directions—*Madame Bovary*. Up until the end she refuses to confess not so much her infidelity, but that she lost her handkerchief at the market, and this even after Othello, having spanked her on top of the pillows (this scene is one of the highlights of the performance, a favorite scene of every great Poldevian director), still gives her one last chance before repudiating her. At this point she delivers her justly celebrated reply which we'll quote in English: "What you know, you know." Some have claimed this proves the author of *Othello* was, philosophically speaking, a skeptic; but others, playing on the ambiguity of the Poldevian terms and going back to the quote in the original version, "what thou believest, thou believest," don't agree, and lean toward a sort of rather Lockian empiricism (we won't follow either party into this slippery territory where we'd run the high risk of splitting a shin or two).

By taking his old pseudonym out of mothballs, Alexandre Vladimirovitch had immediately gotten down to work, ready to thwart the machinations of these scoundrels.

"How incredibly clever!" WHortense said, after hearing a rundown of the plan. "It's going to work, I'm sure of it; can I go on sleeping with Gormanskoï and refining his jealousy? That way it'll torment him all the more afterward."

It was at that moment that Augre began to have his *suspicions,* and soon got *jealous.*

"Yes, of course, my pet," he said, his face expressionless, "go right ahead! He's not your father!"

But he started furiously searching for some way of finding out whether she was cheating on him.

Chapter 32

Suspicion

Suspicion is everywhere. This novel is pervaded by an air of suspicion. Augre suspects WHortense, but he's not alone with his suspicions.

For instance, Hortense's suspicion arose as follows: the jealousification campaign waged to Othelloize Gormanskoï presupposed that the latter and WHortense would be meeting. But they weren't in Le Havre anymore; Gormanskoï saw Hortense as Hortense even though he continued to live at his mother's. Augre had to go to great lengths to get the two of them together. So he sent Hortense a note, supposedly from Gormanskoï, requesting that she buy him something in another section of Queneau'stown. (No, this isn't going to work; what will Gormanskoï say later on when Hortense shows him what she's come back with? How annoying that I've lost that piece of paper where I synopsized this chapter, and now my plans have slipped my mind; OK, I'll wing it.)

So he sent Hortense an anonymous note that said: "Come over here and see if I'm there. A friend who has your welfare at heart." ("Over here" was an address in the suburbs that entailed a two-hour round trip for Hortense |yes, but then how is Gormanskoï going to be at home, if Hortense isn't? How really annoying to lose track of your notes like this when you're a novelist; I don't think I did lose that piece of paper, just misplaced it, it's probably somewhere in the pile of mail I haven't answered since starting to write the book; never mind, I'll wing it|.) Hortense, intrigued, got her handbag and left. Shortly after, Gormanskoï, for some reason or other, arrived at Hortense's. And right on Gormanskoï's heels, WHortense.

However, Hortense, having forgotten something (what? whatever could she have forgotten? When I asked her, after the book was finished, she told me she didn't remember; never mind, I'll just let it be), came back. She almost ran smack into WHortense. She spotted her, toyed with the idea of going head to head, dropped it, and hid behind a hazel tree that was passing by (I don't mean that the hazel tree was in motion; hazel trees, which are wise [hazel nuts are the fruit of wisdom, any good Celt will tell you as much], don't move around like that; they stay right where they are; don't make me write nonsense, what I mean [damn, losing your notes is such a nuisance!], something perfectly sensible, namely, that in relation to Hortense, **relative to Hortense** who is at this moment our point of reference [what's this? A piece of paper with "shift of reference" written on it? Could it be . . . No, just some dumb pun: "shift of reference" mustn't be confused with "shift of reverends," which alludes to the replacement of church pastors. Into the waste basket!] the hazel tree seems to be moving). Why is that? It too has just been stricken in turn by **suspicion.**

When Hortense discovered in Acrab'm's company that Gormanskoı had spent time in Le Havre with a pseudo-Hortense, she realized this implied the inevitable existence somewhere out in the world (but from which one?) of a quasi-Hortense outwardly indiscernible from her (her reasoning was flawed, since as we know WHortense has six *physical* defects compared to the Hortensian prototype [three can't be named]; but she reasoned by analogy with herself), and which the Prince couldn't therefore recognize as "pseudo" without any outside clues.

That he had slept with her was definite since he spoke to her about it ingenuously, making certain requests which she granted gladly but which were all new to her, and consequently could have come only from that particular source. She had been jealous, but since her conversation with Laurie and Carlotta in Chapter 29, her jealousy had waned.

182

And now the other one was back. However, while looking at her, Hortense sensed that there wasn't the slightest possible doubt that the other wasn't herself. Gormanskoï couldn't go on over to the bistro of love and order "another" sometimes, and at others, "the same," and receive identical Hortenses. Without reaching any final verdict about the tramp's moral character, one thing was for sure: she wasn't Hortense! So then, how could Gormanskoï have thought—and still keep thinking—that there was just one of her? She had a suspicion.

She suspected that Gormanskoï knew perfectly well that Hortense wasn't for real, that she was a fake Hortense. He was cheating on her with her double! He was probably laughing inside! He was probably getting some rotten pleasure out of it! That's why he was so calm when Acrab'm and she, in the innocence of their hearts, in the newfound innocence of their hearts, confessed what they thought to be their transgression (and it certainly was one, for Acrab'm). She hit her boiling point in a flash. She was literally radiating fury, a radiance equivalent to that of at least 2200 new candles, which is nothing to laugh about once you recall that a square centimeter of base matter, heated to the melting point of platinum, radiates in a direction perpendicular to its surface only at an intensity of 60 "candelas" or new candles. She was on the verge of pouncing upon them, catching them redhanded and having it all out. But she got hold of herself; she had to make sure no stone had been left unturned. And once sure, she would plot her revenge. She went off to a park bench between a linden and a Judas tree.

At this point Alexandre Vladimirovitch came to sit beside and completely reassure her.

And then Ophelia,
And then Carlotta,
And then Laurie
added their confirmation.

(From Hortense's diary) Alone, I went over to sit on a bench in the large park in front of Sainte-Gudule Cathedral. I was reassured about the Prince; that is to say, about his love; he loved me, no doubt. He was seeing somebody else, the Fake Hortense, but not on purpose, I can accept that; he couldn't tell one from the other—again, no problem. But I was really forced to wonder (whether the Author likes it or not) whether he was any different from the other two after all. Outwardly he looked perfectly princely, his coloring was delightful, but what else did he do in the world but go around princifying? And what am I going to do afterward? Become Premier Reigning Princess? Suffer Acrab'm's bleating eyes (and if I write "bleating eyes" here, I write "bleating eyes," I'm doing just as I like) and spend all my time running away from Prince Augre under the watchful gaze of Alexandre Vladimirovitch? The prospect leaves me rather cold.

(Note written the next day.)

I've just re-read the pages of my diary where, far from the eyes both of the Author and the Poldevians, I confided my true thoughts. It's frightening. Such drabness! Such mediocrity! Is that really me? It's time to leave Poldevia and get back to myself.

(Later.)

An even more horrible thought just occurred to me; what if the Author had discovered this diary after all. . . .

Chapter 33

Say: "33!"

The next morning Hortense was busy having tea, plus brioches and croissants from Groichanskoï's bakery, in the kitchen with Ophelia, Laurie, Carlotta, and the Author, who had come from his hotel (The Zealand Ambassadors Hotel, a stone's throw from the princely palace), when a majordomo of the Prince came in and announced that a gentleman was asking to see her. He introduced himself as the theater master of the Reigning Prince, sent by the Reigning Prince to help her learn the role she'd be playing for the nontransfer of power ceremony.

"Mademoiselle's fiancé," he explained, "is Premier Prince Presumptive of Poldevia; the day after tomorrow he must succeed the Reigning Prince, who must step down from his throne according to the tradition inaugurated by General Bourbaki on reaching his fifty-third birthday. The Reigning Prince steps down from the throne while the Presumed Prince steps up. This is what's called transfer of power. Therefore the ceremony will be transformed into a nontransfer of power ceremony. The Reigning Prince will nonstep down from his throne and Prince Gormanskoï will nonstep up. During the ceremony, a short play will be performed. That's why I'm here," concluded the theater master (in whom we recognize, despite his disguise as a Congolese canoe, Augre the Demon Prince!).

"And what am I supposed to say?" Hortense said.

"Hardly anything; a few words that don't make much sense, in English. Shall we begin?"

"Let's," easygoing Hortense answered.

("That girl's a real airhead," Carlotta whispered in an aside, "can't she tell him to get lost? We've got loads of stuff to do. We're going to the swimming pool," she added for the Author's benefit. "We have a date with a very friendly little Poldevian girl, Ariane." [Question for the Reader: you've already met Ariane, the little blushing Poldevian girl, but in which chapter?])

AUGRE, alias the THEATER MASTER: " 'Will you come to bed, my lord?' Repeat."

HORTENSE: "Will you come to bed, my lord?"

THEATER MASTER: "Alack, my lord, what may you mean by that?"

HORTENSE: "Alack, my lord, what may you mean by that?"

THEATER MASTER: "Then heaven"—new line—"Have mercy on me!" etc., etc., up until: "Kill me tomorrow; let me live tonight!"

HORTENSE *(who has trouble breathing):* "O Lord, Lord, Lord!"

CARLOTTA *(who doesn't understand English, to the Author):* "What are they carrying on about?"

THE AUTHOR: "First, she's got to ask her lord if he's going to come to bed; next, apparently after the lord in question's answer, she asks him again what he meant by that; this goes on for a short spell and at last she says: 'Then heaven'—new line (which shows they're reciting verse)—'Have mercy on me'; etc., etc., . . . ending with 'Lord, Lord, Lord,' which in this case we should understand as 'O God, God, God.' "

CARLOTTA: "Grim stuff!"

LAURIE: "Worse than you think!"

For what the phony theater master intended to make Hortense say was plain and simply the last lines of dialogue uttered by Desdemona during the course of the fatal night in Act 5 in Shahkayspear's version of the drama, grimmer by far than its Poldevian counterpart (where, let's remember, Desdemona just gets spanked by Othello)! Carlotta became indignant; she thought he should get his face smashed in; instead they opted for an underhanded approach, because such was the advice of Alexandre Vladimirovitch, who arrived at that juncture (*Note for the benefit of reviewers:* "juncture": that point in time at which something or someone arrives; synonym: "at this moment"; see *then*). He pointed out that he hadn't taken the pseudonym Hotello for nothing, and that he would be the one playing the role in Gormanskoï's place; there was nothing to fear.

Hortense, however, wasn't as easily reassured. She had the distinct sensation of being smothered at the end of the rehearsal, and she was afraid that some black magic was at work which Alexandre Vladimirovitch wouldn't be able to counteract. Laurie suggested that too much was enough, they should make for the airport, hop a plane, and go home.

"I'm fed up with Poldevia. Let's hit the road, Jack," she said.

"And never come back," Ophelia answered, assenting with her whiskers.

"See you later, alligator," said Carlotta.

"After while, crocodile," Laurie concluded.

Hortense agreed they were right, but she didn't want to leave without her One True Love (but she actually did want to leave). They were deadlocked.

And just then Hortense started coughing. They felt her forehead, it was feverish. She had the Poldevian flu.

They had to call a doctor.

The doctor arrived.

He made Hortense lie down in bed, and then he asked:

"32 + 1?"

"33."

"31 + 2?"

"33."

"30 + 3?"

"33."

"28 + 5?"

"33."

"27 + 6?"

"33."

"24 + 9?"

"33."

"22 + 11?"

"33."

"18 + 15?"

"Uhhh . . ."

"18 + 15?"

"33."

"Fine; relax; let your mind go blank; just take it easy."

The doctor sounded her chest for a long time, lifted her pull-over, and for another long time explored her breasts with his hands; he pressed his left ear against her left breast for a long time, and for a long time his right ear against her right breast, then the reverse; he had her turn over on her stomach, lifted her skirt, pulled down her panties, and for a long time probed her buttocks, turned her over on her back, spread her thighs and examined down around there for a long time. "This is a pretty thorough examination," Hortense thought. "This is just what my cousin Emile used to do playing doctor when we were ten years old." Finally he got up, nodded his head, sat at the desk, took out a prescription pad and a Social Security form from his briefcase, wrote one prescription which he handed to Alexandre Vladimirovitch, and another, which he gave to Hortense.

Alexandre Vladimirovitch gave him a Poldevian *shling;* and he left.

Hortense took the slip of paper absentmindedly, read it, blushed, and cried: "This is going too far!" She handed it to Carlotta, saying: "Read it out loud for us."

Which Carlotta did. "What does it mean?"

"It means that the doctor's no doctor; he's Prince Acrab'm disguised as a doctor so he could come over and feel me up: and after telling him that it was all over, that I wanted nothing more to do with anything."

"He *is* a handsome young man," Laurie said, "as handsome

a young man as your Gormanskoï."

"True," Hortense said, "but things are complicated enough without him. And plus, really, he's too nerdy; a sonnet, can you imagine; listen to this:

SONNET (THIS IS A SONNET)
FOR HORTENSE

A DISKETTE IS OUR HEART
BY LOVE INITIALIZED;
WE TAP ON THE KEY MARKED
FOREVER OUR PWET'S ART.

THE COMMAND'S NEVER SAID,
TWENTY YEARS SAFEGUARDING
MEMORIES OF OUR SPRINGS
IN THE MacINTOSH OF OUR HEADS.

ALAS, A BUG FROM THE BLUE
HAS EATEN OUR HARD DISK
(PRONOUNCE THE SOUND: "OUUU");
THE PROGRAM'S IN DISREPAIR:

"SYNTAX ERROR" SAD YELL
FLASHES LIKE A DEATH KNELL
IN OUR SOUL'S SOFTWARE.

"It's a mystical sonnet," Hortense said. "He's a computerist by religion."

"A sonnet," Carlotta said, "a sonnet; how medieval!"

"It's the kind of thing they used to write before we were born," Laurie explained.

Ophelia, who had composed one sonnet cycle dedicated to Carlotta, and a second, a little shorter, dedicated to Laurie, blushed; but nobody noticed because of her fur. The Author . . . (but we aren't here to discuss the Author's private life).

"Well, what do you know!" Hortense said. "I think I'm all better!"

Love, even when unrequited, is a great healer.

(*Hortense's diary*) Too much is enough. And it's more than just a little too much, it's out and out too much. Saddling me with Acrab'm like this (and I'm being polite)! I don't think I'm going to be able to stand much more of this. There aren't thirty-seven ways around this: either people quit ridiculing me, or I'm out of the novel. It'll be hard on the Author, no doubt; but my mind's made up. Authors don't like for their heroines to grow up, it's true; they find this the most difficult thing in the world to admit; but this is *my* life here, these are *my* adventures; he'll just have to get used to it. And at any rate, I'll only be taking showers for the rest of my stay in Poldevia.

Chapter 34

The Meeting on the Faiwmurr Pass

Introductory scene. The cemetery of Queneau'stown on a rather nippy early morning; Gormanskoï and Acrab'm, wrapped in vast greatcoats, wearing schapskas *on their heads, join the two grave diggers; it's very cold, and consequently the scene is much abridged. The second grave digger hands Gormanskoï a skull; it used to belong to the Anglican (the Prince's denomination) pastor, Yorickskoï.*

GORMANSKOÏ-AIRT'N

Alas, poor Yorick! I knew him, Acrab'm, a preacher of infinite sermons, an excellent expert on the Bible.

Enter, twenty-eight lines ahead of the edition of Hamlet *in the New Cambridge Shakespeare (again, because of the cold), Alcius, Gertrude, lords, servants carrying a coffin, Eltare.*

GERTRUDE

Lay her i' th' earth,
And from her fair and unpolluted flesh
May violets spring!
Sweet Ophelia,
Farewell.

Acrab'm starts in terror. The Reader becomes frightened.

Prince Airt'n shows no emotion and remains silent: he doesn't say "What, the fair Hortense?" *nor* "I loved Hortense. Forty thousand brothers could not with all their quantity of love make up my sum, whether it comes from Reimann, from Stieltjes, or from Lebesgue. . . ." *(Hortense doesn't have forty thousand brothers.) He keeps quiet. Alexandre Vladimirovitch, glimpsed behind a tombstone, takes aim on Alcius with his Winchester.*

The coffin opens and Ophelia appears, alive and kicking; she takes in the scene with her surprised, innocent, and offended eyes (she's cold); she recognizes Gormanskoï, who sat down on a tombstone, and jumps up on his lap; she purrs (to get warm). Alcius and Gertrude suddenly get agitated with agitation. End of scene.

"Should I?" I wondered.

"How about waiting for the last, thirty-seventh chapter?" I asked hesitantly.

"It's already crammed full," I answered.

"Now, then?"

"Now."

"Right you·are," I congratulated myself.

Reigning Prince Alcius's "Hamlet-Hatmel" plot was almost diabolical enough to be worthy of the Demon Prince himself. But Prince Airt'n, after taking Alexandre Vladimirovitch's advice and dumping down the toilet the contents of the bottle supposedly filled with "6 Rose Bourbon" (the best Poldevian brand) which the Reigning Usurping Prince Alcius had given him for Christmas, only pretended to be completely taken in and *to be acting against his will.*

The cemetery scene should have been more or less the final one (a phony brother for Hortense, Eltare, had even been hired for the duel which would have proved fatal for Airt'n). A teddy bear containing a hypnotic substance had been delivered to Hortense, who slept with it to keep herself warm during those long winter nights without her prince; and, that very morning, the order "Ophelia!" rang in her ears, and should have ended up with her jumping into the water and letting herself be placed asleep for a hundred years (Alcius didn't want her to die, simply to get her out of Poldevia and separate her from Gormanskoï) in the coffin in Eerlosni Castle.

The poor Prince would have discovered a Sleeping Beauty Hortense after opening the box and exclaiming, following the text of the play: "What! the fair Hortense?" etc. But what Alcius had not counted on was that the hypnotic command to lie down in the coffin and go to sleep for one hundred years could be addressed only to somebody answering to one specific name: "Ophelia!"; and it was Ophelia who had answered! That makes one! But what Alcius also hadn't counted on was that the hypnotic command to lie down in the coffin and to go sleep for one hundred years had *no effect on cats!* And that makes two.

He was defeated. Gormanskoï got up from Voltairskoï's tombstone where he had been sitting, took Ophelia in his arms, said good-bye with these words to Alcius: "Until tomorrow, at the transfer of powers ceremony," and then left, accompanied by Acrab'm, Alexandre Vladimirovitch, and the two grave diggers, his bodyguards (don't tell me you hadn't guessed that the two grave diggers were Gormanskoï's bodyguards).

The Reigning Prince had failed; he had only one card left up his sleeve: his alliance with Augre on the latter's draconian terms. The interview between the two accomplices—one, dictator of Poldevia; the other, of Poldadamia—took place on Faiwmurr Pass in the mountains separating Poldadamia from Poldevia (a frontier which exists, by the way, at all points in the two territories). Alcius's princely train climbed along the single track joining Queneau'stown to the Faiwmurr Pass, precipitously zigzagging above the torrent bed where in the past the Pascher Brothers painted those marvelous religious scenes, jewels of the Poldevian pre–Renaissance, now housed in the capital's museum. Meanwhile, simultaneously but in another compossible world. Augre's princely train was crossing the same distance ("same" but "another," since it was in Poldadamia), and came to a stop in the no-man's-land beside Alcius's cars.

The two princes opened their respective compartment windows and started negotiations. Negotiations is a strong word. In fact, from first to last, Augre decreed his wishes and Alcius was pretty much forced to give in to everything. For one moment he did try to act high and mighty by raising his spiral stool so he could look down with scorn on Augre; but the latter spun his even higher, and spinning higher by turns Alcius was the one who wound up smashing his face; after that he no longer put up a fight.

The consequences of this interview (where plans for world conquest were also drawn up) will be felt in Chapter 37.

After the pact was concluded and sealed with the blood of the two protagonists on parchment (Alcius fainted at the sight of blood; he had to be brought around to affix his signature), they went to refresh themselves with a cool drink of *apfelsaft*. The apples in the Faiwmurr region are the most famous in Poldevia. Gertrude had quite a start on seeing WHortense; but she regained her composure and the two ladies talked fashion.

Chapter 35

Jealousy

We've now reached what will be the shortest chapter.

Augre's plan hinged on gradually kindling jealousy in Gormanskoi's soul, transforming him into Othello; and the poison would be distilled into his ear by WHortense. The events would follow very closely the Poldevian version of *Othello* in which the equation Iago=Desdemona would oblige WHortense herself to provide the Prince with the grounds for jealousy; she would take the opportunity to strut her stuff with the Prince and show more fiery enthusiasm than she ever admitted to Augre (which Augre, increasingly jealous, knew about through his spies). But Augre's jealousy doesn't concern us here.

This scenario is the mirror image of the one concocted by the Reigning Prince, inspired by *Hamlet*. In reality, contrary to popular belief, evil totally lacks imagination. Evil, says Father Risolnus in his grand opus, the *Prolegomena rhythymymorum*, is either metrical (i.e., fated to perpetual repetition) or chaotic, disorganized. It can never break free of these two poles of arhythmicity. Only good is rhythmical; which is why music, that is, rhythm itself, rhythm incarnate, is good. Evil, when all is said and done, cannot understand good, because neither meter nor disorder can give the slightest clue about rhythm; but good encompasses evil, since rhythm encompasses meter as it does chaos, and surpasses both. It follows that a villain who embodies evil in human form—if he's not in parrot form, or a victim of quotaholia—is animated by a Brownian movement. You can be either original, remarkable, rhythmical—or damned. All roads to hell look the same, but every road to paradise is different in its own way.

What foiled the plans of the conspirators (who would have been vanquished in any case, but no doubt not as easily, by Alexandre Vladimirovitch with the help of the Author and the other good characters) is quite simply their own lack of imagination, which typifies evil creatures. For when Gormanskoi's suspicion had changed into jealousy (having the word, he was going—in accordance with the theories of the Poldevian linguist, Gorgiaskoi—to create the thing), continuing as he did to see Hortense embodied in WHortense, he started spying on her; and having been forced (as before) to act things out according to the play, he was the one who turned into Iago, and WHortense-Desdemona found herself on the defensive, in an awkward position. The result was that with each act following in quick succession (since the transfer of power ceremony was just around the corner) they reached the fatal scene in no time at all. Without understanding what was happening to her, WHortense found herself across the pillows, getting spanked like almost no other actress playing the role of Desdemona in the Poldevian *Othello* had ever been spanked before (the buttocks of actresses playing Desdemona in the Poldevian *Othello* are insured). After which, she got kicked out the door, sent home to her mother's, expelled from Poldevia and forbidden to ever set foot in the land again; Alexandre Vladimirovitch, with a swipe of his claw, scarred her buttock, thus permanently disqualifying her from playing Hortense.

After the spanking was administered and Gormanskoi came back to his senses, he felt cured of his jealousy, even a little ashamed about the spanking, for which he apologized to the real Hortense, who knew the whole story, but kept quiet. (I don't know, even now correcting the proofs, whether Hortense ever made up her mind to reveal the existence of the Fake Hortense to the Prince.)

Chapter 36

Bathing One Last Time with Hortense

I'm not talking about Gormanskoï's last bath with Hortense, or near Hortense, or in sight of Hortense, or even perhaps the Reader's one last bath with Hortense (who knows?), but about the very last bath in the book. And what we're actually dealing with is a shower. Why a shower? Because a shower, being vertical, is more apt to allow those in attendance to keep their wits about them, which is necessary in a chapter on difficult, lofty themes. Baths are horizontal; when Hortense takes a bath she lies down; this position is inappropriate for this episode. If the Reader still hasn't had his fill of seeing Hortense, he can either turn back to the earlier chapters where we have, in several stages, described a complete Hortensian bath, or activate his memory, or if he absolutely insists, for personal reasons, on seeing Hortense horizontal, he can mentally rotate her in her shower $\frac{\pi}{2}$ in the positive direction (which will put her on her back; if he wants to see her other side, he should proceed in the negative direction). You can take your pick (a rather good description of Hortense, although not in her bath, can be found in another novel by the same author, *Our Beautiful Heroine,* available from a rival publisher—*Publisher's note*).

Hortense was in the shower, soaping herself down, before getting dressed for the transfer of power reception at Eërlosni Castle. She was giving herself a good soaping, zealously and methodically as always, but mechanically, without those inspired moves that made her self-soaping so stimulating for the Prince, her lover. This was because Hortense was pre-occupied, worried, about to make a serious decision which the announcement of Ophelia, Laurie, and Carlotta's imminent departure rendered all the more urgent. Carlotta had agreed to put off going back to the City for one day in order to try out her New Year's Eve outfit for the Bruyères-les-Amoriques party on the Poldevians. (The strapless long-line bra needed adjusting, since it had this tendency to drop at the wrong moment. "Your boobies are too tiny," Laurie said. "I am as you made me," Carlotta answered. "She looks just fine the way she is," Ophelia said, trying to sneak away with the thread.)

The three princes entered the bathroom. Added to the Author, the Reader, Ophelia, Alexandre Vladimirovitch, and the Publisher (hey, what's he doing here?), it made quite a crowd for a single bathroom (true, it was large). The princes had donned their ceremonial costumes, replete with hexacorn hats: one was red, the other blue, the third green. Hortense glanced at them coldly. She really felt like telling two of them: "Leave!" (and she almost felt like telling all three: "Leave!"; yes, she *almost* felt like) so that the only man left would be the one granted permission to see her in the shower; but which was the right one? She felt the anguish of Prince Augre's evil exhalations, for he was surely among them; they reached her but without allowing her to determine their exact point of origin. She felt that good Prince Acrab'm, who wasn't *the* good prince, was making calf eyes at her, but which one had a pair of calf eyes? She couldn't tell. It hadn't escaped her attention that Prince Airt'n's color was red, Acrab'm's green, and Augre's blue, the color of treason. But given the compossibility of worlds and their unpredictable effects (for her), could she trust this criterion? There was always Alexandre Vladimirovitch; one glance at Alexandre Vladimirovitch and she would be set; but that struck her as an admission of weakness unworthy of her.

She opted for the *Partimen Method.*

The Partimen Method was invented by Prince Arnaut Danieldzoi in the thirteenth century. It was a foolproof way of distinguishing true from false in matters of the heart. You ask a question, to which one of two possible answers must be given, and this answer decides the issue.

"After dark you arrive," Hortense said to the red, blue, and green Princes, "at the Beast's Castle; a repulsive creature is mistress of this castle; she welcomes you and offers the Noble Kiss. 'Do you want,' she asks, 'to give me a kiss?' What's your answer?"

"Yes," all three said without hesitating.

"I might have guessed," Hortense thought (Why?—*Author's query*).

"You give the Noble Kiss; the Beast, who was a gorgeous young lady cast under a spell by an evil enchanter, is immediately changed back into the gorgeous young lady she really was all along. And she says: 'You've rescued me, I'm yours; there are two possibilities: either I remain beautiful by day in the eyes of all, of the Reigning Prince and the Court, and I turn back into the Beast by night; or else I remain the Beast by day, in the eyes of all, of the Reigning Prince and the Court, and I become beautiful again by night for you alone.' When do you choose for me to be beautiful?"

"By day," Blue said.

"By night," Red and Green said.

"Leave," Hortense said to Prince Augre, the traitor in blue, who had been showing his true colors all along. "You're unmasked."

While she rinsed off her suds, the Reader got an eyeful (of Hortense, not the suds; nothing's too good for you—*Author's note*). She stepped from the tub and into her bathrobe.

"Now it's both your turns. Green Prince and Red Prince, tell me what you think, which choice must be defended? 'So victorious is the shrewd lover / That he reaches his lady's bed / And so honors she her lover / That she charges him to choose / A sweet task and take with a kiss / At the start or when he parts / Tell me which is your desire / Which you would prefer / Upon

199

parting or at the start?' "

"If I understand correctly," the Publisher said, "the lady's proposing something simple: either he chooses to kiss her right away, or he waits a little bit; is that right? You've got to be clear; I'm just thinking about the Reader."

"I suppose so," Hortense said, "I suppose so."

The two Princes answered; their answers were different and Hortense recognized Gormanskoï (who answered what?). True Love always has the last word.

All the Princes had gone to the castle for the ceremony. Hortense, the Author, Alexandre Vladimirovitch, Ophelia, Cyrandzoï, Carlotta, and Laurie followed, as soon as Laurie was ready.

"I'm late," Laurie said to the Author, who was looking at his watch, "but putting pressure on me'll get you nowhere; it'll make me even later."

We have a little breather before the finale. We've all noticed Hortense's hesitation when the three Princes inopportunely barged into the bathroom (an incident the Publisher used as an excuse for meddling in affairs that were none of his business). Had Hortense changed?

She had been wondering this herself while taking one of her last baths (which the Reader missed, busy reading another, far less interesting book than ours, *H*****'* G*****; too bad). "Have I changed?" she wondered as she watched the tub water swirl down the drain. "Am I still the same person as the one who took a bath yesterday in this same tub? Is it the same tub? Even if yes, it's of absolutely no interest; I don't care whether it's the same tub or not. But has my love started to fade, have I stopped loving? Have I thrown the baby of love out with the bathwater of Heraclitus?" she thought, increasingly worried, increasingly philosophical.

Then she went into the salon to ponder the problem out loud, interrupting a marathon game of Kings between Laurie, Carlotta, the Author, Alexandre Vladimirovitch, Ophelia, and Blognard and Arapède (Blognard's wife and Arapède's mother had gone off to visit the Leeiff Tower; Father Risolnus never played cards). Laurie and Carlotta cheated, slipping all the bad cards to the Author who didn't have a clue what was going on. Alexandre Vladimirovitch showed preferential treatment to Ophelia, his dear, newfound daughter.

"If I question myself," Hortense thought out loud, "I'll say: 'I'm me' but can I be so sure? Are you all certain about your identities?"

"Yes," Carlotta and Ophelia answered in unison. "Besides," Carlotta said, "Laurie and I aren't Poldevian; we're just passing through; it's got nothing to do with us."

Laurie said she wasn't certain she had an identity; consequently, she couldn't relate to the question about changing.

"And what about you, Al. Vl.?" Hortense said.

Alexandre Vladimirovitch said he was a Poldevian Cat Prince, consequently Pyrrhonic to the same degree he was Byronic. The only thing he could say was that he didn't know whether he could rationally justify the fact that he thought that nobody knows anything. Blognard was pondering the problem posed by the transfer of power ceremony and kept silent. Father Risolnus said that it was a simple question of marking polyrhythms; the rhythms of the real Hortense couldn't get confused with any others; a rapid analysis of her wavelettes proved this.

Lastly, Arapède paid tribute to the excellence of Alexandre Vladimirovitch's positions. He pointed out that the hexacompossibility of Poldevian worlds posed serious problems for the theory of identity in these worlds. For it was clear that Hortense had changed worlds several times and at any one or another given moment had found herself in at least three different worlds. She perhaps must face not so much the Riddle of Lichtenberg's Knife (that would be going too far, such a change was too coarse) but instead the Riddle of Theseus's Boat.

201

Which means what, exactly? Well, that in passing from one world to another, we could for instance picture her being instantly decomposed into her component particles (infinitely small, a la Robinson, if you like, it's not important), then recomposed no less instantly.

"Now, Theseus's boat," he said to Carlotta, "is placed in dry dock for repairs; the planks are taken out one after the other and replaced with brand-new ones. Theseus arrives, compliments the shipyard workers, and sets sail on the wine-dark sea. But the planks from the original boat weren't thrown out; they were used to construct an identical version of Theseus's first boat. So which one is Theseus's boat?"

"That's just what I was saying," Carlotta said, "we're not Poldevian, right?"

Hortense resisted. "I'm me, just me, all the time," she said. "I'm me, first of all; and next, I'm in love; and no sophistry, no skeptical Cat Prince, no Sextus-Empirician police inspector, no Evil Demon, will convince me that I'm wrong in thinking that I'm in love, and that I am me.

"But I sure am sick and tired of Poldevia!"

Envoi and Chapter 37

In Which the Novel Comes to an End and the Characters Go Their Separate Ways to Tend to Their Own Personal Affairs

There is a crush of people on the vast esplanade, a half-bowl dug out opposite the entrance to Eërlosni Castle, the reconverted former gasworks that looks like a stack of six pancakes decorated with hexacolored pipes. Everything comes in groups of six in Eërlosni, for it's the nerve center of Poldevia, thus of the Hexarchy and its six worlds.

The crowd is rushing forward to attend the transfer of power ceremonies. Prince Airt'n, Premier Prince Presumptive, is going to succeed his uncle and second spouse of his mother, the Unlawful Interim Reigning Prince of Poldevia at Home and Abroad, Alcius. This doesn't suit the latter's purposes, and so he's sulking in his ceremonial yellow costume. This doesn't suit Augre's purposes either; he's dressed in a magnificent blue that sends shudders of disgust through everyone who's not in his camp: dictator of Poldadamia against the will of the people and the dynasty, he ousted Prince Acrab'm, in green, brother and friend of Airt'n, who is wearing a melancholy smile because of his impossible love for Hortense. It's not raining outside, just misting; the clouds are jostling each other in order not to miss anything.

The crowd of guests presses its way inside where it finds the Court, its Ladies and Noblemen, the constituent bodies, the different oils (theological rapeseed, financial peanut, artistic olive, journalistic and televisual castor, scientific walnut, peasant and worker elbow grease). There's the Gratin (Dauphinois of Commerce, of banks . . .); there's High Society, Low Society . . . the Sixth of Society; everybody who matters in Poldevia and Poldadamia; and the foreign ambassadors (noticeably present are Sir Clerihew, the representative of Her Majesty from Great Britain, who arrived with his wife, née Trent, at the wheel of his Bentley barouche). All of Poldevia, all of Poldadamia is there: cats, ponies, snails, human beings. There are so many people you wind up noticing none of them at all.

The crowd is motley, dazzling. The six colors of the Hexarchy, the six colors of the six worlds, the six colors of the Poldevian rainbow—red, purple, orange, blue (boo!), yellow, and green—shine everywhere, upon suits, dresses, in the chandelier light, the glasses served by the waiters.

The Author enters, followed by the Reader, out of breath as he tries to catch up. He rubs his hands together, his book will soon be finished, he's going to be able to take a vacation; he sings:

> "When the end of the novel comes
> on the page
> We'll all have to say good-bye . . ."

Carlotta, Laurie, and Ophelia make their entrance; there are murmurs; two redheads at once, this was some celebration! Laurie is wearing her black tuxedo, Ophelia her soft light-colored fur; Carlotta is in her New Year's Eve party dress for Bruyères-les-Amoriques (Jim Wedderburn's holding the stole just in case; but the strapless bra is staying put). You can hear fingers snapping as they pass. A few young Poldevians are making the sound, just a handful of young Poldevians, not everybody, that would be tacky and obtrusive; a few young mutually distinguishable Poldevians in the Kevin Costner mold or . . . (No! I beg you, not Gregory Peck! no!) or like Gregory Peck in one of his early movies. Some are snapping their fingers for Laurie, others for Carlotta; still others for Ophelia.

Alexandre Vladimirovitch is invisible.

Misters T. and T. are hiding in the corners.

Father Risolnus is drinking while keeping an eye peeled for little Ariane.

Inspector Arapede and his mother, Inspector Blognard and his wife are dressed to kill. But Blognard and Arapede quickly slip off; they've got things to do; they've gone to meet the police chief of Queneau'stown, Efhocu. They got to put final touches on a plan of action.

Carlotta crosses the room, hanging from Cyrandzoi's neck; the sound of snapping fingers follows in her wake.

Hortense enters, looking beautiful. A murmur begins to rise: "Beautiful Hortense, beautiful Hortense."

The transfer of power ceremony begins; they dispense with the speeches. Alcius is on his throne; he looks out of sorts. He glances around distractedly; he seems to be waiting for something that's not happening. At the foot of the throne are the six Princes.

At last the moment has arrived. The ecumenical archbishop of Queneau'stown takes the scepter from the hands of the U. I. R. P. P. H. A. . . . He motions him down from the throne. The latter hesitates, then resigns himself.

The archbishop hands the scepter to Prince Airt'n.

The latter takes it with sovereign nobility.

He mounts the thirty-seven steps of the throne (the last two are double).

He sits down. An immense clamor spreads through the room. The new Reigning Prince reigns.

Just then there occurs something like an infinitesimal maelstrom (in time), a chaos, a topsy-turvy jumble; everything clashes together, gets mixed up, confused, and flies back into place.

We've changed worlds. Everybody winds up the way they were before, everything lands on its paws, **except,**

all the Poldevians have switched colors (only the Poldevians; rest assured, the redheaded females are still redheaded, and Carlotta's dress held steady).

You say to me: "Fine, so what?" So what! You say "so what" to me?! Well, let's just see about this now:

Accompanied by the police chief Efhocu, Blognard goes up to the six Princes. The chief is going to utter the fateful words: "Prince Augre, by virtue of the powers vested in me and in the name of the Reigning Prince, I place you under arrest," but which one is Prince Augre? Nothing sets the six Princes apart from each other but the color of their ceremonial costumes (and their trademark, the sacred snail on the left buttock, whose six distinguishing dots are arranged in idiosyncratic patterns; but they too turn with the worlds). And these colors have switched around! But how? Of course, the police chief knows; but he doesn't want to take the plunge; he is acting under orders; this Efhocu is a devious character. He turns to Blognard with a look at once inquisitive and sardonic.

"What should I do?"

Blognard could ask Hortense, who by now is perfectly capable of distinguishing between the three. He could ask Alexandre Vladimirovitch who has just appeared on his shoulder. But he has his reputation to defend.

In order to understand how Blognard, in his genius, tackled the solution to this problem, you must know three things: namely, the first, the second, and the third.

The first is the legal questions posed by Blognard, which the Princes should answer according to their nature: with the **truth** if they were **good;** with **falsehood** if they were **evil.**

The second is that Prince Acrab'm, as a result of his adventure with Hortense, wound up being traumatized and shattered. And one of the effects of this traumatic experience exacerbated by his lingering dizziness after he changed worlds (which caught him by surprise right in the midst of painfully recalling Hortense's most poignant charms) was that he no longer knew **whether he was good or evil** (a fact Alexandre Vladimirovitch just whispered into Blognard's ear (Blognard's such a wonderful name for a detective, don't you agree?—*Author's note*). But the others had remained intact.

The third—which is actually just a reminder of something you ought to know—is that the Hexarchy's hierarchy assigned **first rank to Reigning Prince Airt'n, the lower third rank to Prince Acrab'm, and the even lower fourth rank to the Demon Prince Augre.**

Now you have all the clues. Blognard addressed the three Princes, requesting the others to withdraw: remaining behind were **the Purple Prince, the Orange Prince, and the Green Prince.** Next he requested Carlotta to step forward (an exercise in logic is always good for a high school student planning to major in math).

Blognard's questions for the three princes: (a) Is the Purple Prince of higher rank than the Orange Prince? (b) Is the Purple Prince of higher rank than the Green Prince?

The Green Prince's answer to question (a): No.

The Orange Prince's answer to question (b): Yes.

Blognard asked Carlotta: "Which one is Acrab'm?"

Carlotta whispered the answer in his ear; it was correct.

Blognard then said to Carlotta: "And what if I were now to ask the Purple Prince which of the two Princes, Green or Orange, is of higher rank, what would he answer?"

Carlotta told him.

Blognard finally turned to the Green Prince and asked the third and last question: (c) Is one among you evil?

And the Green Prince answered: "Yes."

It was over. Blognard and Carlotta knew. Hortense already knew. Alexandre Vladimirovitch had always known. The Author was hoping he hadn't made a mistake. And what about the Reader?

Be that as it may, Police Chief Efhocu went up to the criminal and said: "Prince Augre, by virtue of the powers vested in me and in the name of the Reigning Prince, I place you under arrest."

But no arrest was made. Augre gave a secret signal and the accomplices he had stationed in the six corners snapped into action by flinging water bombs, stink bombs, and itching powder. Fleas and horse flies were simultaneously released and got the better of the cats and ponies respectively. The emergency reinforcements of snails arrived too late. The conspirators rather swiftly gained control of the premises. It was a coup d'état, and a successful one.

What Alcius had been waiting for on his throne became clear; the coup d'état was supposed to take place *before* the transfer of powers. But Augre had pulled a fast one on Alcius, who felt he had aged twenty-three years in a flash. From now on his only title would be Ex-Reigning Prince. But his wife Gertrude consoled him. They would retire to some island; she would write her memoirs; and he would do the cooking. He was thoroughly comforted, and so now we can leave him behind.

In the disorder of the coup d'état, Ophelia, Carlotta, and Laurie were separated from Hortense. All three were arrested shortly afterward in the palace to which Hortense and the Prince had never returned; the next day, along with the Blognards and the Arapèdes, Jim Wedderburn, the Reader, and the Publisher (hey, what's *he* still doing around here?), they had one and all been politely but firmly placed on the first flight out for the City, where they returned, tired but happy to see an end to their adventures.

END

Post-end

My sincerest apologies, I forgot to tell you what became of Hortense, her Prince, Cyrandzoï, Alexandre Vladimirovitch, a snail whose name we'll not reveal, and Prince Acrab'm, now good again.

A few days after the coup d'état perpetrated by Prince Augre that had toppled the legitimate government of the Hexarchy, a barouche, drawn by six strong Percheron racehorses, pulled up after dark at a lonely vineyard estate out in the Poldevian scrubland, north of Villeverte-le-Crémade. From the vehicle emerged our six outlaws, our fugitives, attempting to escape the secret police of the Usurping Demon Prince who were in pursuit. With British passports (five fake and one authentic) furnished by Sir Clerihew, Her Majesty's ambassador, they had come looking for precarious and temporary refuge with the Prince's old nurse, in retirement here. Hortense leaned on Gormanskoï's arm as she got out of the barouche; she had gladly forgiven him for his jealousy; she was setting out once again, in love (conditionally this time), toward an uncertain future which would be—she had firmly resolved—a long, long way from Poldevia.
In the farmyard a little girl was singing:

> "Why'd you dye your hair, my lovely maid;
> Why did you, what a nightmare,
> I really preferred your old shade,
> I really preferred your old hair."

And Gormanskoï was swept by old memories.

The old nurse came out to welcome them herself despite her rheumatism. A cheerful fire of old vine shoots was blazing in the rustic fireplace. She greeted everybody politely all around, kissed Hortense on her four cheeks (left right, left right), hugged Gormanskoï in her arms (not for a second did she get him mixed up with Acrab'm; she didn't even seem to spot the resemblance).

"How big you are, my little one," she said. "I won't go gathering figs after you, *biétaze!*"

(This is fresh evidence—if any further were needed—of the deep kinship which exists between Poldevia and Provence, where this is a traditional saying.)

They sat down to eat. They had a *escoudeyetdzaia* with six kinds of starches: polenta, rice, potatoes, pasta, broad and string beans. The nurse worried over their appetites: "Eat, eat! You need all your strength to escape those bandits; but these youngsters are standing on ceremony! Alexandre Vladimirovitch, don't put your paws on the table. Cyrandzoï, your pony shoes!"

The snail munched on his fennel.

Later, candlesticks in hand, they went to spend the night in large, freshly made beds scented with lavender and thyme. They fell asleep to the sound of the wind in the wooden shutters.

Very early the next morning, long before dawn, they had to be off; Augre's henchmen were hot on their trail. We'll leave them here; we'll wave "bye-bye"; we'll catch sight of the snail climbing onto the rear window, who will give us a little wave back with his left horn; and Alexandre Vladimirovitch's whiskers, the smile he leaves behind on parting, to reassure us; we'll watch the barouche disappear into the first light of day, climbing along the cypress-lined slope, up toward the hillside, the mountains, the nearby frontier. We'll go home, climb back into our nice warm beds.

(Will they be overtaken and captured? Will they escape? You'll find out when you read the sequel to these adventures in *Lady Hortense;* the Reader still hasn't caught up with the Author, whoosh!)

And this is the Final End.